He pressed his ▓▓▓▓▓▓
hers and kisse ▓▓▓▓▓▓
should kiss a woman. ▓▓▓▓
respect and tenderness and min▓
blowing desire.

She made the sweetest sound. Her fingers threaded into his hair and pulled him closer still.

The kiss went on and on. Deeper and deeper, then slower and sweeter.

He would have given most anything to make love to her. But she was vulnerable right now. He wouldn't take advantage of that. Instead, he lay down beside her and held her close. Let her feel how much he wanted her. Let her know that he was there for her.

Whatever the cost, he was in for the duration.

Dear Reader,

Thank you so much for choosing my book.
This story represents a major milestone for me.
Small-Town Secrets is the thirty-second COLBY AGENCY
story. I am so proud to be a part of the Harlequin Intrigue
family. I hope you will enjoy this and next month's
COLBY AGENCY installment, as well as the final book
in the trilogy, coming in September.

This year marks a couple more very important milestones
as well. For one, this is Harlequin Intrigue's 25th
anniversary. Imagine, for twenty-five years the Harlequin
Intrigue line has been bringing readers a breath-stealing
ride with suspense, thrills and, of course, romance. Readers
never have to wonder what they'll get when they pick up
an Intrigue story. From the high-octane action, the gut-
wrenching suspense, the most wicked villain to the sweet
and sizzling connection between the hero and heroine,
Intrigue always delivers as promised. Harlequin Intrigue
offers fast and furious reads each and every month!

Also, this year is Harlequin's 60th anniversary! No other
publisher has consistently brought romance to readers in
every possible setting and with every imaginable scenario
the way Harlequin Books has. Whether a small-town girl
racing toward her future with an international tycoon or a
sexy billionairess seeking refuge in the arms of a big, strong
cowboy far away from her metropolitan home, Harlequin
has it covered. Every book, every month features a new
and interesting twist on the tried and true as well as in
cutting edge, previously uncharted territory. Escape—that's
what Harlequin has given readers for more than half a
century.

So, turn the page and escape with me!

Best,

Debra Webb

DEBRA WEBB

SMALL-TOWN SECRETS

TORONTO • NEW YORK • LONDON
AMSTERDAM • PARIS • SYDNEY • HAMBURG
STOCKHOLM • ATHENS • TOKYO • MILAN • MADRID
PRAGUE • WARSAW • BUDAPEST • AUCKLAND

To my amazing editor, Denise Zaza, and to the readers
who keep the Colby Agency alive.

Recycling programs
for this product may
not exist in your area.

ISBN-13: 978-0-373-69412-9

SMALL-TOWN SECRETS

Copyright © 2009 by Debra Webb

ABOUT THE AUTHOR

Debra Webb was born in Scottsboro, Alabama, to parents who taught her that anything is possible if you want it bad enough. She began writing at age nine. Eventually, she met and married the man of her dreams, and tried some other occupations, including selling vacuum cleaners, working in a factory, a daycare center, a hospital and a department store. When her husband joined the military, they moved to Berlin, Germany, and Debra became a secretary in the commanding general's office. By 1985 they were back in the States, and finally moved to Tennessee, to a small town where everyone knows everyone else. With the support of her husband and two beautiful daughters, Debra took up writing again, looking to mysteries and movies for inspiration. In 1998, her dream of writing for Harlequin Books came true. You can visit Deb's Web site at www.debrawebb.com to find out exciting news about her next book.

Books by Debra Webb

CAST OF CHARACTERS

William Spencer—A former child-advocacy attorney turned Colby investigator.

Dana Hall—Part of her childhood is missing—the part where her twin sister was murdered.

Victoria Colby-Camp—The head of the Colby Agency. Victoria has always been unstoppable, but can she stop the threat to her granddaughter?

Jamie Colby—Victoria's only grandchild, Jim Colby's daughter.

Jim & Tasha Colby—Victoria's son and daughter-in-law.

Lucas Camp—Victoria's husband and closest friend.

Ian Michaels & Simon Ruhl—Victoria's seconds-in-command.

Chief Gerard—Brighton's chief of police. Who is he covering for? Too many inconsistencies in the investigation adds up to a botched job.

Carlton Bellomy—Dana's former neighbor. A man who may know what happened that night.

Lorie Hamilton—Former cheerleader and Miss Popular. Was she afraid of a little competition?

Ginger Ellis—Former cheerleader turned waitress. Was reality too hard for her to accept?

Patty Shepard—Former cheerleader turned mother and wife. Did her need for revenge push her over the edge?

Samuel Henagar—Former school janitor. He liked looking at the young, pretty girls. Where was he the night Dana's sister was murdered?

Mr. and Mrs. Hall—Dana's parents. Was it more than the loss of his daughter that sent Mr. Hall over the edge?

Donna Hall—Did Donna die in her sister's place? After all, Dana was the one with all the enemies.

Chapter One

Chicago
Inside the Colby Agency

"She's the perfect choice."

Victoria Colby-Camp reclined in her leather executive chair and considered the man who had spoken. Simon Ruhl was one of her most committed colleagues. He and Ian Michaels were her seconds in command. She trusted both implicitly. If Simon had concluded that Merrilee Walters was the perfect choice, then she was without doubt the ideal choice.

"Excellent." Victoria nodded, punctuating the announcement. "Ian, you'll follow up with Spence as to any possible legal ramifications in hiring an investigator who is hearing impaired?"

"I will." Ian had left the final decision up to Simon. Still, he had reservations about Merrilee's ability to fulfill the requirements of the position, but nothing conclusive to veto bringing her on board. More a feeling, he insisted in previous discussions.

"If Spence finds no legal precedent of concern, then we'll move forward," Victoria offered.

Simon and Ian exchanged a look. One that said the decision wasn't nearly as cut-and-dried as Victoria suggested.

"What am I missing?" They had been over all the issues more than once. No one assigned to the agency's Elite Reconnaissance Division had voiced a problem with this potential staff addition. The final approval was Victoria's, but Simon's and Ian's agreement was paramount to her decision. If there was still a problem beyond the one Ian had mentioned, she needed to know.

Ian clasped his hands in front of him, an uncharacteristic move for a man whose absolute stillness even in moments of extreme tension proved intimidating to most. "My gut instinct hasn't changed," he finally said. "The Colby Agency has made its reputation on employing only the best. The most highly trained, the most honorable as well as the most physically able. Rarely have we stepped outside those parameters. Miss Walters is deaf—a challenge that puts her at a considerable disadvantage in normal situations."

Ian held up a hand when Victoria would have interrupted. "I am fully aware that she reads lips with inordinate skill. The hearing impairment is not my actual concern, though there will be clients who won't understand that Miss Walters is fully capable. My concern," he added with a pointed look at Victoria, "is the seemingly relentless need to prove herself that she appears to possess. Her record at Nashville Metro is solid evidence of a potential problem. She may very well take risks that put both her and the client in danger."

True. However, Victoria never allowed the evaluations of others to wholly guide her. Not that she doubted Metro's assessment, but that was only one side of the story. Nonetheless, Ian's point regarding Merrilee's penchant for diving headlong into a situation without regard to caution held merit. Victoria was surprised that Ian felt so strongly about this particular characteristic. More often than not, he was an avid proponent of those who took the initiative to set themselves apart from the rest.

"Are you recommending we don't move forward?" Victoria really hoped that wasn't the case. Since she'd conceived the idea of an agency reconnaissance division, her primary goal had been to ensure the team was made up of members from every walk of life. After all, those who went missing came from all backgrounds. She wanted her team to be able to fit in anywhere. No one understood the needs of those physically challenged better than one who carried that burden.

The Colby Agency's Elite Reconnaissance Division had one mission: find the missing. Victoria, with Ian's and Simon's help, had organized an elite team thus far. Like William Spencer, a former child advocacy attorney. And though, as Ian pointed out, Merrilee Walters was considered a bit of a rogue by her peers and superiors back in Nashville, she had definitely proven what she was made of over and over again.

Bottom line, Victoria wanted Merrilee on their team. But all seated in Victoria's office at the moment needed to be on the same page.

"I'm recommending," Ian explained, "that we hire Miss Walters on a conditional basis with an extended probationary period. We'll see how it goes for a time before putting her in the field."

"Fair enough," Simon agreed. "I'm convinced you'll grow to respect her ability to assess a situation before plunging in as well as her skills."

"Time will tell."

Obviously Ian was far from convinced. A good deal more than Victoria had realized. And she was relatively certain his reservations had more to do with the woman than the opinions of others. But, as he said, time would tell. "Very well. We're all agreed then."

With a nod from each man, both of whom Victoria respected tremendously, the meeting was adjourned. Simon would move into negotiations with Merrilee and Ian would follow up with Spence.

Before the door could close behind Ian and Simon, Mildred Ballard, Victoria's personal assistant, stepped into the office. "Victoria, you received a call from Dave Glenn."

Victoria smiled. She hadn't spoken to Dave in ages. "Put him through."

"Unfortunately he was on his way to a meeting." Mildred glanced at the note in her hand. "He wanted to know if you could have lunch with him at Tony's Pub around one."

Victoria checked her wristwatch. It was eleven now. She had to pick up her granddaughter from pre-school at twelve-thirty. With Jim and Tasha out of the country, Victoria generally brought Jamie back to the office with her for the afternoon.

"Don't worry," Mildred said, reading her mind, "I'll pick up Jamie and keep her out of trouble. Go to lunch," she urged. "You've been spending too many lunches in the office lately."

That was all too true. Victoria would very much like to catch up with Dave. "You're absolutely right. Do I need to leave him a message to say I'm coming?"

Mildred shook her head. "All you have to do is show up. He's already made the reservation for the two of you."

That was Dave all right. Always completely sure of himself. But then, he'd trained with the best: Lucas Camp. Victoria's husband was a man who never took no for an answer. Lucas and Dave had been friends since childhood. Lucas's unwavering determination had long ago rubbed off on the other man.

"You don't have another appointment until three-thirty," her loyal assistant added. "Take your time. Enjoy catching up."

"Thank you, Mildred."

As the door closed, Victoria found herself sighing. She'd suffered so much loss and pain in the past. Taking for granted a moment of her wonderful life now was out of the question. She had the most amazing husband whom she loved more deeply every day. She had her son and he was well and happy. And she had a beautiful granddaughter. Not to mention the agency continued to thrive.

Basically, Victoria had it all.

She deserved this happiness. She intended to enjoy it to the fullest.

At one when Victoria entered Tony's Pub, Dave Glenn waited at the bar. As she approached, Victoria took a moment to consider the man. The same age as Lucas, his hair had long ago paled from blond to a lustrous white. Age had not diminished his intimidating stature or his proud military bearing. He was still a force with which to be reckoned.

As if he'd sensed her presence, he turned on the bar stool to face her. Sharp blue eyes lit with the smile that broadened his lips in welcome.

"Victoria, I'm glad you could come." He set his glass aside, slid off the stool and reached for a hug. "It's been too long."

Victoria relished the embrace of a dear friend. It really had been too long. Drawing back, she assessed the rugged face that spoke of decades of too many secrets and too little R&R. He needed to slow down and enjoy life. Lucas had told him so many times. She wished Lucas were here now.

"Dave, it's so good to see you."

He reclaimed his glass and ushered her toward the dining room. "Our table is waiting."

When Victoria had settled into a chair and Dave had done the same, she sent a pointed look at his drink of choice. "It's a little early for scotch, isn't it?" She'd never known Dave to indulge in the middle of the day. "Are we celebrating something?"

Dave peered into his glass a moment before meeting her gaze. This time there was a bleakness about his expression. "I'm old, Victoria." He gave his head a little shake. "The job is finally beginning to get to me."

A frown tugged at her brow. Though both she and Lucas had seen this coming, the statement was uncharacteristic of the man who never failed to present himself a pillar of strength and determination.

"Our chosen fields can become burdensome at times." She knew this all too well. But to her knowledge Dave had not suffered the personal loss Victoria had experienced. Perhaps this was nothing more than the long overdue realization that his work could not continue to have priority over his personal life. "Is Catherine doing well?"

Dave managed another smile, but this time it didn't reach his eyes. "She's tired of spending so much time alone." A halfhearted shrug lifted his shoulders. "She's found other ways to occupy her time."

Victoria ached for the man. A breakup was never easy, but he and Catherine had been married for twenty-five years. Clearly he was devastated. "I'm sorry to hear that." What else was there to say? Sorry, however, seemed a pathetic offering.

Dave pointed to his glass as the waiter paused at their table. "And a white wine for the lady." When he'd returned his full attention to Victoria, he said, "It happens. I suppose I should have been paying better attention."

A gentleman to the end. It would have been so easy to blame everything on his wife's inability to appreciate his commitment to his country. "Perhaps you'll find a way to work things out."

"Perhaps." He finished the last of his drink. "How's Lucas?"

Victoria's lips slid into an automatic smile at the mention of her husband's name. "He's well. He's away on business for a few days. Thankfully he's home more often than not, but he continues to work in an advisory capacity when he's needed."

Dave gave her one of those looks that said he knew exactly what she meant despite her understanding words. "You remind him that retired means precisely that. I knew he wouldn't take himself completely out of the game."

"Now that's the pot calling the kettle black," she teased, opting to lighten the moment.

He laughed, but the sound was dry. The waiter arrived with their drinks, and they placed their meal orders.

"And Jim?" Dave asked. "He's still doing well with his shop?"

"Yes." Victoria's chest tightened with pride. "The Equalizers are doing exceptionally well. Jim is happy helping those who don't seem to fit in anywhere else. He has a knack for resolving the unsolvable."

"Like father, like son," Dave offered, his gaze distant as if he were remembering his days with Lucas and Jim's father, James Colby.

Victoria sipped her white wine, mainly to restrain herself from asking the question pressing against her sternum. This small talk was nice, but it failed to camouflage a glaring ulterior motive for today's impromptu invitation. Victoria's instincts were on point. Something was very wrong. Something more than her old friend's personal problems. Dave was not himself by any means.

He lifted his glass, apparently thought better of it and lowered it back to the table. He exhaled a heavy breath. "There's something I need to tell you, Victoria, and I'm not sure how to go about it."

"Don't mince words with me, Dave. We've known each other far too long for that. Say what's on your mind." Lucas was deep in negotiations related to national security. Jim and Tasha were on safari in Africa. She'd heard from them only two days ago, just before they left for an extended excursion into a remote jungle location. Whatever Dave's news, it couldn't be related to her family.

Dave propped his forearms on the table and rested his gaze heavily on hers. "You know how the world of intelligence operates. I don't have to spell it out for you. We trawl for information. Sometimes in the worst possible places, dredging intel from the worst possible characters. That's how the job gets done."

Victoria nodded. Like Lucas, Dave worked in intelligence. Lucas worked directly for the government as an advisor while Dave was employed by a government contractor. And he was right; the job could take them into gritty places.

Uneasiness stiffened Victoria's spine. "You've heard something of a personal nature that concerns you." It wasn't a question. She knew perfectly well where this was going.

He nodded. "You know if it was insignificant, I wouldn't bother passing it along."

She did. "Does this information involve the Colby Agency?" No matter that the Colby Agency maintained a prestigious reputation, enemies were made. It was part of the business.

"No. Not directly."

"Me, then." She would much prefer he simply get to the point.

He nodded. "Yes. I attempted to trace the information beyond my source, but I was unsuccessful. So, be advised that I have no tangible evidence to back up what I'm about to tell you. All I have is a rumor. A rumbling of discord so to speak." Those assessing blue eyes bored into hers. "But this source is solid. Precautions need to be taken."

"Have you spoken to Lucas?" It suddenly struck Victoria as quite odd that he didn't go to Lucas first. But then, she didn't know the nature of the information he was about to pass along.

"I couldn't reach Lucas this morning. And I feel this shouldn't wait."

She inclined her head in question.

"My source," he began, "indicated that there's an operation in the final planning stages to take down Lucas where he is most vulnerable."

Victoria's breath stalled in her chest. "You're right. Precautions do need to be taken." She didn't have to add that this, of course, wasn't the first time nor would it be the last that someone attempted to seek vengeance on Lucas. He'd made more than his share of enemies while working with the CIA. But no one was better at taking care of himself than Lucas. Dave was well aware of that fact.

Victoria understood with complete certainty that the other shoe was about to drop.

"Whoever has set this plan in motion intends to use you to get to Lucas."

Victoria considered the warning. "I'll beef up my personal security, particularly while Lucas is away." Nothing she hadn't faced before. She knew the proper steps to initiate.

Dave shook his head. "It gets worse, Victoria."

A blast of adrenaline seared through her limbs. "Don't keep me in suspense."

"I don't know many of the details, but I do know that the plan supposedly involves kidnapping your granddaughter."

Tentacles of fear constricted around her chest.

"This could be nothing more than grumbling from someone you or Lucas have brought down. Blowing off steam and tossing around threats," Dave suggested, his voice uncharacteristically soft and soothing. His eyes reflected just how badly he'd hated to pass along this information. "But considering what happened in the past, I felt you'd want to hear this as soon as possible whether or not it is warranted."

Victoria knew that Mildred and Jamie were at the office. She'd touched base with Mildred en route to meet Dave.

That didn't stop Victoria from reaching for her phone.

She couldn't take any chances. Not with her granddaughter. She had to be sure.

Victoria couldn't live through *that* kind of pain again.

Chapter Two

Dana Hall reminded herself to relax. The hustle and bustle of the Colby Agency lobby had kept her distracted at first. But now, forty-five minutes later, things had grown quiet and her anxiety had started to build.

It was almost half past four and her appointment had been at three-thirty. Dana glanced at the receptionist. She'd apologized repeatedly for the wait.

But it wasn't the wait that had Dana's tension escalating. It was second thoughts.

Was she making a mistake by starting this? Should she leave the past in the past? She was twenty-nine years old. What difference did it make now? Learning the truth wouldn't change anything. Her sister would still be dead. In reality, the truth would change nothing at all that mattered.

What did she hope to accomplish?

Dana closed her eyes. Peace. That was her goal. She couldn't live with the uncertainty or the nightmares. Not anymore. The longer this went on, the more detailed and intense the nightmares became.

It was time to have closure.

To know the truth…whatever the cost. Whatever it accomplished.

"Ms. Hall?"

Dana looked up, then stood. "Yes."

The older woman who'd called her name smiled. "I'm Mildred Ballard, Victoria's personal assistant. I apologize for the wait. Victoria can see you now. This way, please."

Dana followed Ms. Ballard along a long, lushly carpeted corridor until they reached a smaller, but every bit as impressive, lobby. Ms. Ballard indicated the double doors across the carpeted expanse. "Go right in, Ms. Hall. Victoria is waiting."

As the older woman took her seat behind her desk, Dana gathered her fleeing courage and walked toward the double doors. She was doing the right thing. No question. She couldn't continue to live this way. She had to know the truth, and this was the only way.

The Colby Agency came highly recommended. Not one she'd looked into had a better reputation. The agency's long-standing in the business and priority on discretion sealed her decision.

Dana opened the doors and entered the elegantly appointed office of Victoria Colby-Camp, head of the prestigious Colby Agency. The woman in charge stood in greeting.

"Ms. Hall, welcome to the Colby Agency."

Dana summoned a smile. "I appreciate your personal attention to my case, Ms. Colby-Camp."

"Call me Victoria." The head of the agency directed Dana to one of the chairs flanking her desk. "I give my personal attention to all our clients."

Dana's spine stiffened with continued uncertainty as she lowered into the upholstered chair. This was good, wasn't it? Assuredly she couldn't complain about not getting her money's worth if the woman in charge saw to Dana's needs personally.

Victoria reclaimed the seat behind her desk. "How can my agency help you, Ms. Hall?"

"Dana, please." Dana took a breath. "I suppose I should start at the beginning." When Victoria nodded, Dana continued. "I'm from a small town in Indiana. Brighton. My family and I lived there until…my sister was murdered when I was thirteen. My sister and I are…*were* twins. I'm looking for closure. I'm hoping the Colby Agency can help me find it."

Victoria leaned forward and penned a note on a file that likely had Dana's name on it. "A tragedy such as that is difficult to move past. I'm sure you were all devastated."

Dana managed a wooden nod. "At first we tried to move on with our lives, but considering the murders went unsolved, staying in Brighton was impossible."

"Murders?"

Dana swallowed tightly. "My sister was one of three victims murdered that fall. All three were local children. They died within mere days of each other. The whole community was devastated."

Sympathy etched itself across Victoria's brow. "Does the case remain on active status or has it been officially closed?"

Dana shrugged. "My mother receives calls from time to time whenever some new-to-the-force deputy decides to take a look at the town's most infamous case. Nothing has ever come of it. The case has been cold for nearly a decade now."

"But," Victoria offered, "you need to know the truth. Closure, as you said."

Dana's heart pounded harder with each passing moment. "Yes." The word was scarcely a whisper. She needed the truth. She needed to face the past or put it behind her once and for all. So far she'd been able to do neither on her own nor with the help of a psychiatrist.

Victoria braced her elbows on her desk and

steepled her fingers. "Losing a family member is difficult under any circumstances," she said gently. "But losing a twin is like losing a part of yourself."

Echoes of memories whispered in Dana's ears. She moistened her lips. "Yes." It was a nightmare... one that wouldn't end. "My mother and I faced a second blow when six months after we moved from Brighton my father committed suicide." She fought back the emotion that accompanied thoughts of that time. "He blamed himself for not taking better care of us."

After a moment's consideration, Victoria said, "William Spencer is a member of our Recon Team, a division of the Colby Agency created specifically to find the missing. Though the children in this situation are deceased, the truth is missing." Victoria settled a reassuring gaze upon Dana. "The members of this team are the best in the business, Dana. If it's humanly possible to find the truth for you, Spence will find it."

Victoria checked what appeared to be a large desk calendar. "I'd like you to meet Spence. We'll go over the details you remember and determine a starting place and strategy." She reached for the phone on her desk and gifted Dana with another reassuring smile. "You can take a deep breath, Dana. The Colby Agency will find the answers you're looking for."

Dana wished she could take a deep breath… wished that what she felt at those sincere and comforting words was relief, but the truth was, in this case, she felt fear. Fear and dread.

Was she putting the past behind her…or the rest of her life?

WILLIAM SPENCER TYPED the conclusion and hit Print. His first "final" field report was finished. He'd worked six months for the Colby Agency before being assigned a case where he was the primary investigator. Until then he'd done research and assessments. It felt good to be a full-fledged Colby investigator. The work here gave him a sense of accomplishment and self-satisfaction—something that had been sorely missing in his former career as a child advocacy attorney.

He gritted his teeth when he considered the numerous times he'd helped remove a child from harm's way only to have another judge overrule the decision and place the child right back into dangerous territory—typically with his or her own mother or father. The last child he'd rescued using his legal expertise had been returned to his mother and stepfather only to end up dead twenty-four hours later.

Spence had walked away from his firm. Enough was enough. He wanted to be at a place where his efforts actually did some good for the long term. Landing at the Colby Agency was the best thing that could have happened to him, professionally as well as personally.

A distinct buzz drew his attention to the telephone on his desk. Anticipation zinged through him. He pressed the speaker button. "Spence."

"Spence," Victoria said, "I have a client, Ms. Dana Hall, in my office. Could you join us?"

"Absolutely." His pulse quickened as he tapped the speaker button to end the connection and grabbed his notepad and pen. The idea of being assigned a new case immediately after completing his first had him practically sprinting toward Victoria's office.

Grinning, he gave Mildred a little salute. She smiled back at him. That was another thing he loved about working at the Colby Agency. The staff operated like one big family. Since he had no family of his own, not since he was sixteen anyway, the camaraderie filled a long, empty void.

As he entered the boss's office, she announced, "Ms. Hall, this is William Spencer."

The obviously nervous client extended her hand as he approached. "Mr. Spencer," she said softly.

"Ms. Hall." Spence gave her a firm handshake then settled into the chair next to hers.

Dana Hall was blond and petite. She dressed like

most female white-collar professionals, skirt and matching jacket, with a starched white blouse and practical shoes. But it was the big brown eyes filled with sadness and intense worry that overwhelmed her attractive oval face. This was a lady with heavy personal baggage. He knew that look.

Victoria briefly reviewed Ms. Hall's situation. Spence had to admit that he was a little surprised he was chosen for the case considering the three children involved were deceased, more specifically *murdered*. The only homicide he'd been involved with had happened in the present. Personally, he wasn't sure he was the right man for the job. But he trusted Victoria's judgment. She had a reason for asking him to sit in on this meeting. And if she asked him to take the case, she had her reasons for that as well.

"I'd like to be closely involved with the investigation," Ms. Hall said when Victoria had finished bringing Spence up to speed. "The police haven't been very cooperative with any of my past efforts. I need to have an active part in solving this painful mystery once and for all."

"That's understandable," Victoria granted. She turned her attention to Spence. "Ms. Hall's participation will likely be an asset, don't you agree?"

"I do," Spence concurred. Dana Hall would know those closest to the victims and would likely recall the players involved in the official police investigation that followed the murders.

"I'd like to get started as soon as possible," Dana went on to say. "I've lived with this a very long time. It will be a tremendous relief to put this behind me. The sooner the better."

When she spoke of the murders, she avoided eye contact with him, Spence noted. There could be a number of reasons for that, none of which were particularly good. "I'm available immediately." He'd finished the final report on his last assignment. There was no reason he couldn't get started right away.

Dana met his eyes now. "When can we leave?"

Brighton was only a few hours' drive from Chicago. "I'll make the necessary arrangements this evening, and we'll meet here at nine tomorrow morning. We can be there shortly after noon." She nodded and he went on. "I'd like you to compile a list of any relevant details and names you recall that we haven't already discussed. We'll go over those on the way and lay out our strategy."

Dana took an audible breath. "Excellent."

As the meeting concluded, Spence watched Dana interact with Victoria. Every instinct warned him that the lady wasn't being completely open. He had worked with the parents of abused and neglected children long enough to recognize deception on any level when he saw it. This lady was hiding something…something she understood was relevant to the case.

The only question was why.

Chapter Three

Dana hadn't been back to her birthplace in sixteen years.

Nothing had changed.

Brighton was one of those towns where time seemed to stand still.

Her stomach twisted into knots as if her thirteenth birthday had been just yesterday. Images from the party…her and her sister, Donna, wearing silly pink party hats. Balloons floated everywhere and the clown dancing around the room laughed loudly. Dozens of kids played and sang—then everyone had gone home. Night had come and their parents had tucked them into bed. They'd giggled and whispered, too excited to go to sleep. Donna had wanted to sneak out to play in the woods behind their house. Dana hadn't wanted to…but she'd caved beneath her sister's pleading. She'd never been able to say no to Donna.

Dana remembered playing in the damp grass beneath the moonlight. Even now she could almost feel the wet blades tickling her toes…the crisp air whispering against her skin.

But she remembered nothing beyond that.

In the wee hours of the following morning, after an intensive search by local authorities and neighbors, she and her sister had been found deep in the woods behind their home. Her sister was dead, and Dana was disoriented and suffering from mild exposure.

Dana blinked away the past, stared out the car window at the storefronts lining the main street that split the town in half. A left turn would take one to the downtown area where the courthouse dominated a well-manicured square of shops and offices. Beyond the town square were neat rows of streets dotted with brick ranch homes and painted bungalows. A right turn revealed the smaller, mostly rundown homes of the poorer residents. The railroad, light industry and warehouses were interspersed with blocks of tiny duplexes and walk-up apartment buildings. A mile or so outside the town limits lay a stretch of road with a few scattered houses surrounded by big yards and woodlands.

Home.

A place so calm and quiet. Not at all the type of town where one expected to encounter evil.

But it had been here.

And now she was back.

Would anyone suspect her motive?

Or her?

"Dana?"

Banishing the disturbing thoughts, she dragged her attention back to the driver. "Sorry, I was lost in thought."

"Which way to the police department?"

Dana frowned, surveyed the street name on the corner sign and dredged her memory banks for the directions. The last letter her mother had received from the chief had been from the same old address. "Two more red lights then right. You'll see the building on your left, I believe."

William Spencer, or Spence as his colleagues called him, focused on making the turns she'd suggested. Dana studied his profile. He wore his dark brown hair short. His eyes were equally dark. Thirty-six. Law school graduate. She'd looked him up on Google the night before. He'd graduated at the top of his class and gone on to work at one of Chicago's most prestigious law firms. But then the county had persuaded him to give up half his income to work as a child advocacy attorney. Married once. Then divorced. No children. He'd worked at the Colby Agency for only eight months.

Fear that she'd started something she would regret abruptly clasped around Dana's chest. She should just let the past go.

But then she would never know.

"Here we are."

Spence braked to a stop in the parking lot. Dana stared at the long, drab brick building that housed the police and fire departments. Despite the air-conditioning in the car, perspiration dampened her skin as her heart thumped harder and harder.

"Chief Gerard is expecting us."

Dana heard the words Spence said, but the larger part of her attention was focused on the official lettering sprawled across the glass entry she'd last entered sixteen years ago.

"Dana."

Dana gave herself a mental shake and reached for the car door. "Right." Chief Gerard had struggled through the town's first homicide case. Her sister's case.

Sherry's and Joanna's case.

Three victims…three unsolved murders within a week in a town small enough that everyone knew everyone else. Three young girls killed by someone they apparently knew since there were no signs of struggle. How was it possible that no one admitted to having the first clue who that someone was?

Stop. Dana slammed the car door and squared her shoulders. She had to stop allowing her thoughts to go down that path. Focus. She had to focus and let this man—she glanced at William Spencer—do his job. He was the expert here…she was just the desperate client.

And maybe, just maybe, she would learn that she wasn't the one who'd killed her own sister…and two of her best friends.

SPENCE WATCHED Dana Hall closely as they waited for Chief Gerard to finish an afternoon meeting that had, according to his secretary, run over. Dana's emotions appeared to vacillate between high anxiety and extreme dread. The anxiousness was to be expected. The dread, however, surprised him. This was a woman who had clearly suffered for years due to not knowing what really happened to her sister. She'd sought the Colby Agency's help in finding the truth. Despite her insistence that she needed to learn what happened sixteen years ago, she appeared to fear learning that truth.

Spence recognized the symptoms. The woman knew something she wasn't sharing. In his experience with the parents of abused or neglected children, he'd seen those very symptoms time and time again. The burden of guilt weighed on most, even when their instincts urged them to protect themselves. No one wanted to face the reality of what they had done much less the consequences related to the act or acts.

. But what had Dana Hall done besides find herself a victim of the most heinous of crimes?

"I realize," Spence began, "this is difficult."

Dana Hall jumped as if he'd startled her from her thoughts. "I'm sorry." She cleared her throat. "What did you say?"

Seriously distracted. To some degree that was to be expected. "This is difficult, I know," he reiterated. "Revisiting a painful past is never easy. But it's my job to ensure that it goes as smoothly as possible."

She wet her lips. Until then, he hadn't noticed how full they were. Incredibly full and rich in color. She blinked, as if clearing her weary eyes of any emotion that might give away her true feelings. "I can handle it." She glanced around the small office. "I have to."

Was she attempting to convince him or herself?

"Afternoon, folks." Chief Gerard hustled into the office, coffee cup in one hand, a stack of files and papers in the other. "I apologize for keeping you waiting." He shook his head as he rounded his desk.

"Sometimes things get a little hairy even in a small town."

Spence stood. "William Spencer. The Colby Agency," he said as he shook hands with the chief. "You may remember Dana Hall."

Dana remained seated, her gaze locked on to the man in charge of local law enforcement.

"Gracious, young lady." The chief beamed a broad smile. "I haven't seen you in…" His expression fell and sadness appeared as if he'd only just remembered the circumstances of their last encounter.

Dana cleared her throat. "Chief Gerard," she said, her voice faltering.

Obviously shaken, the chief indicated the chair Spence had vacated. "Have a seat, Mr. Spencer." He lowered into the one behind his cluttered desk. "What can I do for you folks?"

This was the moment Spence should have felt guilty for not cluing the man in on the subject of the appointment. But Spence wanted to get his reaction to Dana's sudden reappearance after nearly two decades. He'd definitely gotten one.

"We're here," Spence said, leveling his gaze on the chief's, "to ask you a few questions about Donna Hall's murder."

Chief Gerard looked from Spence to Dana and back. "It's been a long time." He took a sip of his coffee. "Several of my deputies have, over the years, taken a look at the case hoping to find something new. No one has ever found anything. But I'm happy to be of any help if you're set on looking for yourself." He studied Spence a moment. "Your agency is looking into the case?"

That Gerard had blanked his expression told Spence that like all officers of the law, he didn't appreciate a private investigator coming into his territory, nosing around into a case he hadn't been able to solve with his own resources.

Understandable. "That's correct," Spence confirmed. "My agency is aware that your department did everything possible with the technology available at the time." Spence gave a succinct nod. "There are resources available now that might help in solving the case. We'd like to see what we can learn, with your guidance and expertise, of course." Making friends was a far better strategy than drawing battle lines right off the bat.

That seemed to appease Gerard. He relaxed visibly. "I'll pull the files and have them available for you to look at later this afternoon. Around five sound all right to you?"

"Absolutely. That would be very helpful." Spence didn't want to wait for the files. Having to come back to see them gave the chief time to select what would be shared and what wouldn't. Only one way to try and head that off. "Perhaps you could share your thoughts on the case. Anything specific you remember that, in looking back, might have been more suspicious than it seemed at the time?" The chief couldn't very well leave out anything he mentioned before he'd had time to think better of it.

Gerard propped his forearms on his desk and clasped his fingers. He stared at his hands for a bit before speaking. "The people in this town are good folks. We'd never had so much as an attempted murder before…that. When the first two girls were found." He took a deep, burdened breath. "Sherry and Joanna. We were all devastated. Who would do such a thing?" His head moved side to side slow and stiff. "Go into a little girl's room and kill her in her sleep. The calls came in at practically the same time. At first we thought we had some sort of lethal virus. Both girls," he said and glanced at Dana, "were tucked under the covers, eyes closed just like they were sleeping."

He heaved a heavy breath. "Then Dana," he said looking directly at Spence, "and her sister went missing from their beds. We couldn't believe it. How could it happen again? We didn't have the first suspect. No evidence to go on. Nothing. Thank God you were still alive when we found you," he said to Dana.

Dana shifted in her chair as if the weight of his

gaze as well as his words were too much for her to bear. She managed a faint nod.

"According to my research," Spence interrupted the silence that went on a little too long, "the girls weren't sexually assaulted. They were apparently suffocated with something while they slept."

Gerard nodded slowly. "The strangest part was that they appeared to have been attacked by a person or persons who didn't inspire the slightest fear or hesitation. Neither Joanna's nor Sherry's home had been broken into. Dana and her sister were lying on blankets from their own beds in the woods behind their home. There was no evidence of a struggle, none of any sort, not even a suspicious fiber. There was a pillow at the scene in the woods. According to Mrs. Hall, the pillow had come from Dana's bed." Gerard hesitated. "A pillow was the one consistent item at each of the scenes."

Dana jerked as if startled.

"No footprints, other than those of the victims?" Spence prodded. "No indication anyone else had been at the scene?"

"Nothing," Gerard confirmed. "It was as if they'd just stopped breathing or…been suffocated by an invisible assailant. The inconsistency was Donna's head injury. The autopsy results suggested she'd been struck on the head."

"Any speculation on the head injury? Was that a contributing factor in her death?" Spence prodded. Dana hadn't mentioned the head injury.

"She could have fallen and hit her head before the attack," Gerard offered. "There's no way to know."

Dana shot to her feet. "I…excuse me." She rushed from the room.

Spence resisted the urge to go after her. To see that she was okay. But the chief's reaction to her abrupt departure was something he needed to analyze first.

"That poor girl," the man muttered. "Waking up alive and finding her sister dead was just about more than she could take. She wasn't the same after that. You know her daddy killed himself barely six months later."

Who would be the same after that? "I can only imagine," Spence agreed.

"She was suffering from exposure. Shock. She didn't speak for days. And then her mind just blocked whatever she might have heard or seen. Her mother tried everything. Even some kind of regression therapy. But the child reacted so adversely to the treatment that Delores, her mother, was afraid to try a second time. She didn't want to risk the only child they had left. They'd already lost one."

"No one close to the girls was considered a suspect? Nothing they had in common that might have proven a viable link to their deaths?"

Another sad shake of his head. "Four good girls with no enemies. This is a small town, Mr. Spencer. There wasn't a soul I knew then or now—and I personally know every citizen in Brighton—that would have hurt those girls."

"Yet," Spence countered, "someone killed three of them."

OUTSIDE, DANA STRUGGLED to catch her breath. Her heart pounded so hard that the effort was impossible.

How could she have thought for even a minute that she could do this? She had to have lost her mind.

Every word had sent another surge of adrenaline roaring through her veins.

No signs of forced entry or a struggle…just stopped breathing. Suffocated by an invisible assailant…

Dana closed her eyes and tried her level best to banish the images that accompanied the words echoing inside her head.

"Dana? Dana Hall?"

Her eyes snapped open and her attention jerked to the left.

"That is you." A big burly man stepped into her personal space and crushed her in an embrace. "Lord, girl, how long has it been?"

The scent of his familiar cologne and freshly

chopped wood assaulted her nostrils. Dana's head was spinning like a top when he released her.

"The last time I talked to your mama she said you was living in the big city. I'll bet she's real…"

Dana's brain wouldn't absorb the rest of what the man said. Every fiber of her being was focused on his face…his massive frame. Carlton Bellomy. Her former neighbor. He'd lived across the street from her childhood home for as long as she could remember.

He'd found her in the woods…picked her up and carried her all the way back to her house, leaving another searcher with Donna's body.

Dana shuddered. She tried to slow the quaking but that wasn't happening.

"You all right, Dana?"

She blinked, told herself to respond, but it wasn't happening.

When Spence stepped into her line of vision, she sucked in a ragged breath. He looked from her to the man still hovering over her.

"William Spencer," he said as he thrust out his hand.

Mr. Bellomy, his expression cluttered with new worry, glanced from Dana to Spence. "Carlton Bellomy." He pumped Spence's hand.

"I'm a friend of Ms. Hall's," Spence explained. "We're in for a short visit from Chicago."

Bellomy's wide smile slid back into place. "Why I've known this girl and her family since the day she was born. Was their neighbor until they moved away." He made a pained sound in his throat. "After the tragedy."

"Mr. Bellomy," Dana squeaked out, "lived…right across the street."

"Still do," Bellomy said. "I sort of keep an eye on the place. Tack down a loose shingle now and then, keep the grass cut. Stuff like that. I check in with her mama three or four times a year." He set his hands on his hips. "Has your mama finally decided to sell that place? Are you here to get the process started?"

Dana shook her head. Her mother didn't know she was here. She would be extremely distressed if she heard.

"I'm certain we'll see you again while we're here," Spence offered.

"Why sure you will," Bellomy insisted. "I expect you two to come to dinner. Why not tonight?" He looked from Spence to Dana and back. "Unless you already have plans. The diner's 'bout the only place around here to get a decent meal, and it's nothing to compare with the wife's."

Spence looked to Dana for the right answer. "That would be nice, Mr. Bellomy," she managed to squeeze out. Nice was nowhere near the proper description, but she couldn't be rude to the man. Not after what he'd done for her—and her mother—all these years. They hadn't wanted to sell the home that had been in her father's family for three generations. Her mother paid the property taxes, insurance and utilities while Mr. Bellomy took care of everything else. He'd done so for sixteen years. The least she could do was accept his kind invitation.

"Right fine," Bellomy said with a nod. "I'll let the wife know, and we'll expect you folks around six-thirty if that'll work."

Spence said something else…yes and maybe goodbye. Dana wasn't sure if she said goodbye or not as Mr. Bellomy walked away. She could only watch the big bear of a man stride toward his truck. The same one he'd had sixteen years ago.

He would tell his wife Dana was back in town. His wife would tell her friends. By sundown everyone would know.

The only survivor of the town's tragic murders was back.

And just like sixteen years ago, it was obvious that she still wasn't right.

That was another thing Dana hadn't worked up the courage to tell the Colby Agency.

Most folks in her hometown thought that night in

the woods when her sister was murdered had stolen her sanity.

Poor, crazy little Dana.

She wouldn't ever be right again.

Chapter Four

Spence stared into the dusk outside the motel window. The case file had given him crime scene details and backgrounds on the victims but nothing truly useful in the way of suspects.

All three victims had grown up in the area. All three were thirteen. There was no trace evidence that connected anyone to the scenes other than the victims. A single hair belonging to Dana Hall had been discovered on the clothing of one of the first two victims. That had been easily dismissed considering the victim had spent the night at the Hall home the night before her death. The four had friends, teachers and neighbors in common. But not one of those common denominators appeared to have had a motive for committing the crimes. The girls were simply murdered for no apparent reason.

But Spence understood that wasn't the case. No

one was murdered without reason. He'd considered the victims' families and found nothing documented in the way of enemies or recent problems, financial or otherwise. From the reports taken at the time of the murders, each one represented the perfect family. No readily detectable skeletons in the closet. Nothing.

There had to be something the investigation had missed. The fact of the matter was that small-town murder investigations rarely looked very hard at friends and neighbors. Everyone knew everyone else, just as Chief Gerard had said, and it was unthinkable that anyone would commit such a heinous crime. Therefore no suspects.

But Spence didn't know any of these people. Each one was as much a suspect as the other in his opinion. And from what he'd learned so far there was only one way to go about solving this mystery.

Start at the beginning. Nudge the players and watch for the reactions.

He gathered his notepad and pen and headed for the room next door. Dana's room. She had blocked the memories of the events that night. But the memories were there. His goal was to cautiously prod those memories loose from the layers of fear and disbelief that had them buried.

Cooperation was key.

To cooperate she had to get past her fear.

Just like the kids he had worked with for the county. Guide them away from the fear and toward the light of truth.

They still had more than half an hour before they were to arrive at the Bellomy's. Time enough to topple that first domino.

Spence rapped on the door of the room next to his. A moment later, probably after visually identifying who had knocked, the door opened.

Dana Hall looked tired and pale. Interaction with the chief and her former neighbor, Mr. Bellomy, had shaken her. They'd barely arrived in town. His investigation had scarcely gotten out of the gate. If she wanted the truth, she was going to have to rally the necessary courage to go the distance and face her past.

Her lack of cooperation was the one primary stumbling block to getting the job done.

"I'd like to go over a few details with you." He indicated the pad and pen. "We have a little time before dinner with the Bellomys."

She looked past him, then at the pad he held. "I've told you everything I know twice already."

There was some truth to that. She had gone over all she claimed to remember at the agency and then again en route. But there was much more she didn't want to remember, and that was what he needed.

"This part of the investigation can be tedious, but it's necessary if we hope to succeed."

She considered his statement for a moment before relenting and allowing him into her room. That one instant of hesitation, like so many others he had noticed since meeting her, was the part of this mystery that puzzled him the most.

If she didn't want the truth, why come to the Colby Agency looking for it?

He understood how difficult this was for her, but murder was never easy.

As she sat down on the edge of the bed, he settled into the chair at the nearby desk. He placed his pad on the desktop and clicked his pen into writing position. "Start at the beginning."

She licked those plump lips and took a deep breath. "It was our birthday party." She stared at the beige carpet as she spoke. "The party was okay. Mom insisted on having it in spite of what had happened. Not so many kids came, but there was lots of laughing and presents and two cakes. One for each of us."

Her silence dragged on until he prodded, "After the party, what happened?"

"We had a late dinner with our family and went to bed."

"But your sister wasn't ready to sleep." Dana had

consistently maintained that it was her sister's idea to leave the house that night.

She nodded. "It was really late but not late enough to deter Donna. She was always the outgoing one. I was the quiet bookworm." Dana clasped her hands in her lap. "She loved walking in the woods. It was a full moon. She said we'd go to the stream and look at the stars. We did that a lot in the summer."

"But this was October. Had to be pretty chilly."

She nodded. "We bundled up, grabbed a blanket and sneaked out of the house."

"Was this the first time you'd left the house at night without telling your parents?"

A quick shake of her head. "We'd done it a couple times before. We'd meet Joanna and Sherry at the stream. Sometimes Lorie would come, but not that last time."

There was a name he hadn't heard. "Who's Lorie?" This was exactly the reason for going over and over the details. Something new eventually surfaced.

"Lorie Hamilton. She was a friend of my sister's. Most of our friends were really my sister's friends. I guess I was a little too boring for them. Too shy. Too much of an introvert."

Spence could see the remembered pain in her eyes.

"Lorie and my sister didn't hang out together often. Lorie was fourteen and had friends her own age."

Spence hadn't seen an interview report on a Lorie Hamilton in the case file. "Did you mention to the police that Lorie occasionally came to the stream with you?"

A frown furrowed its way across Dana's brow as she bit her lip. "I'm not sure. She wasn't there that night so I probably didn't."

"Your parents never suspected the two of you left the house without their knowledge?" That part nagged at him. But then, he'd grown up in the city. Maybe that was the difference.

"My parents slept upstairs. We used the downstairs den for a bedroom because of my sleepwalking."

Something else he hadn't heard about. "You walked in your sleep?"

"When I was younger. They were afraid I'd fall down the stairs or something. They kept the deadbolts secured…or they did until I'd stopped doing it. By then Donna and I didn't want to move back upstairs. We'd gotten used to the room."

Spence imagined that her parents had beaten themselves up over and over again for that decision.

"What did the two of you do after you left the house?" He guided the conversation back to the details of that tragic night.

"We danced around in the yard. Let a couple of leftover balloons go in honor of Sherry and Joanna, then headed into the woods." Other than lacing and unlacing her fingers repeatedly, she sat perfectly still. "When we got to the stream we spread the blanket and laid down to stare up at the stars."

"Donna didn't fall? Hit her head?"

Dana shook her head. "Nothing like that happened." Inwardly she cringed at the thought that her sister had been hit in the head with a rock…or fallen against one. Why couldn't she remember any part of that?

"What did you talk about?"

She stared at the wall across the room, her gaze distant. "How much she missed her friends. How we couldn't wait until we were old enough to get our driver's licenses. Nothing in particular."

More of that prolonged silence.

"Who fell asleep first?"

Dana thought about the question, then said, "I guess I must have. I could still hear her talking as I drifted off."

"What happened when you woke up?"

Her gaze collided with his. "I don't remember waking up. I told you that."

Her defensive tone also told him she didn't want her claim disputed and definitely didn't want to try remembering.

Move on for now. "Okay. So tell me more about Lorie Hamilton."

Dana blinked. Her frustrated expression relaxed fractionally. "She was a cheerleader. Very popular. Everyone loved her. She and Donna got to know each other when my sister tried out for the cheerleading squad for the upcoming school year."

"They were cheerleaders together?"

Dana shook her head. "Donna didn't make the squad, just third alternate. But Lorie still hung out with her sometimes. Maybe..." Dana chewed her lower lip.

"Maybe?"

"Maybe Lorie felt sorry for Donna because she was like the very last choice even as an alternate."

"What makes you think Lorie felt sorry for Donna?"

"I guess because Lorie only hung out with her when she wasn't with her other friends." She met Spence's gaze once more. "The other cheerleaders, I mean. They kind of stuck together."

"Your sister didn't blame Lorie or feel animosity toward her after that?" It was a shot in the dark, but one the investigators apparently hadn't considered during the initial investigation.

"Of course not." More of that defensiveness. "My sister didn't have any enemies." Dana shook her head firmly. "None of them did."

"But someone murdered them," he said bluntly. "Obviously there was someone who harbored ill will toward all three." Denial was the typical presiding theme in cases like this. No one wanted to believe an enemy, much less one capable of murder, resided among them. Particularly not in a small, quiet town where nothing truly bad ever happened.

The statement had the desired effect. "My sister never hurt anyone in her life. Everyone loved her. She didn't have any enemies any more than Joanna or Sherry did." She pushed up from the edge of the bed. "I should…get ready, I suppose. Can we talk about this more in the morning?"

For a lady who wanted the truth so badly she sure didn't seem to want to go down the path that would lead her to that destination.

Spence stood. "No problem." He moved to the door, but hesitated before leaving. "We should probably get going in about ten minutes."

She said nothing as he exited her room. Somehow he had to get the point across to her that someone hated her sister enough to end her life in a very personal manner. Someone Dana likely knew. Until she was ready to face that harsh reality the memories that might very well lead to a killer would remain locked just out of reach.

Spence had gone easy on her until now. Tomorrow he would push a little harder. He'd worked with children who suppressed unpleasant memories. Prodding them gently but consistently was essential.

He was surprised therapy hadn't unearthed a flicker of recall. Then again, Dana could be working overtime to keep the memories at bay. Nothing he hadn't seen before.

Whether she fully realized it or not, she was the key element to finding the truth. Chances were, she knew the killer.

His job was fairly straightforward: guide and prod her to that end.

All he needed was her cooperation.

DANA SECURED the safety latch on the door. Her hands shook. She fisted her fingers and fought to regain control of her emotions.

How long would it be before Mr. Spencer recognized her deception? How was she going to survive going to dinner with the Bellomys? Right across the street from her childhood home?

She wanted to find the truth. Out there. She gazed at the door, her mind conjuring the images of her hometown. She wanted to learn that some stranger just passing through had committed these atrocities. There had to be a way to accomplish that goal without giving away her deepest fear. Her dreams were just that…dreams. They didn't mean anything. Not really.

But what if they were real? What if she was…

No. She refused to even think it. She'd loved her

sister. Joanna and Sherry had been her sister's best friends. Had always been nice to Dana and let her tag along. She couldn't have hurt them.

Was that the reason she couldn't remember? Her therapist had said what happened that night was obviously too traumatic for her mind to allow her to remember. Was that yet another indication of her guilt?

Dana fished into her purse and checked her cell phone. Her mother had tried to call three times. Apparently Mr. Bellomy or Chief Gerard had informed her that Dana was here.

Not good.

She tucked the phone back into her purse. How long would it be before her mother showed up here to try and urge her to go back to Chicago?

The phone on the bedside table rang and Dana jumped. She dragged in a deep breath and counted to ten, releasing that breath slowly. She had to pull herself together. Mrs. Bellomy had probably already spread news all over town that she was here. It was an easy guess where Dana would be found since the Goodnite Motel was the only motel in town. Another sharp ring shattered the air.

If her mother was calling, Dana would just have to deal with it. She couldn't have her showing up and attempting to persuade Mr. Spencer to rethink helping her. If that happened, Dana had to make her understand that she wasn't walking away until she knew the truth.

The whole truth.

Steadying herself, she crossed the room and picked up the receiver. "Hello."

For several seconds dead air reverberated in her ears, mimicking the rush of blood already roaring there.

"Hello."

"You should go back to Chicago, Dana. The past should stay in the past. Otherwise…you'll be sorry. We'll…all be sorry."

The click that followed confirmed that the caller had severed the connection. Dana stared at the receiver in her hand. Her heart thumped hard against her sternum as the words seeped through the denial swaddling her brain.

Female. Vaguely familiar somehow. But…none of the people who had once known her would have made that kind of veiled threat. Would they?

Unless…it was someone who knew what happened that night.

Someone who knew that to find the killer, Dana only need look in the mirror.

Chapter Five

Dana managed to get through dinner without falling apart. She'd noticed Spence watching her on too many occasions to count. Everyone had been watching her. Mr. Bellomy. Mrs. Bellomy. She'd picked at her food, that was true. But how could she eat? That phone call. The voice. The warning.

Being here…in the house…right across the street was very nearly more than she could bear.

She'd scoured her memory banks in an attempt to put a name and face with the voice of the caller. No luck. She was sure Spence and the Bellomys had also observed her distraction. The only thing good about being distracted was that she had been able to block a good deal of the conversation regarding her childhood.

Picture-perfect. Her family, the town, all of it was nothing short of Norman Rockwell ideal. The words, the images they invoked, were like knives sliding deep into her flesh. She could scarcely abide hearing.

This was crazy.

She followed the others onto the front porch for coffee. Dana had come here to learn the truth and already she was ready to cut and run like the coward she was. That was the real truth here. She was a coward.

"It was a more carefree time back then," Mrs. Bellomy said as she settled into a wooden rocker. "Never locked our doors. We all sat on our front porches in the evenings. Even in October most evenings were still warm enough to do that."

A shiver danced along Dana's spine, as if to deny that assertion. Images from the past flickered in front of her eyes…urging her to look back. To see. Dancing through the woods. The damp grass…

She blinked, forced the nerve-jarring images back into that locked compartment that never really opened for her except in her dreams. It was as if her mind had segregated her memories, allowing only a haunting teaser of those she wasn't permitted to see. And only in her sleep.

"Without any children of our own—" Mr. Bellomy picked up where his wife left off "—we enjoyed watching the girls play in the yard across the street. They were like our surrogate kids."

Dana's attention settled on the dark house beyond

the expanse of pavement making up Waverly Street. The home where she'd once lived still looked mostly the same. The paint was faded. The lawn was freshly mown, probably for the last time this season. But it was the windows, black holes against the weathered siding, that taunted her.

Empty.

Abandoned.

Like her life.

Hard as she'd tried to pick up the pieces after surviving college, she just hadn't been able to feel anything. She couldn't allow even one personal connection. She'd muddled through somehow. Existing. Until the nightmares started in force. She'd had the occasional one all along but not this night-after-night punishment. They stole what little focus she managed. Made her feel out of place in her own skin.

How was she supposed to go on without doing something? Without knowing?

But the thought of looking back, finding the truth, terrified her. Yet, she knew with all her heart that she had to do exactly that.

"Dana?"

She snapped from her disturbing musings. "Excuse me?" She'd completely missed whatever had been said. "I'm sorry I was…just thinking."

That everyone seated around the porch stared at

her with something akin to concern sent heat flooding her cheeks.

"I was saying that we should probably be going," Spence repeated. "We've taken up enough of our generous hosts' time, and we have a full day ahead of us tomorrow."

Dana nodded jerkily. When Spence stood, she followed suit.

"Thank you for a lovely meal," he said.

"We'd love to have you come by again," Mrs. Bellomy said to Dana. "We've missed you. It feels like old times having you here."

Dana managed a smile. Her lips quivered.

"Let me know if there's anything at all I can do to help," Mr. Bellomy said as Dana and Spence descended the steps and walked toward his car.

Dana scarcely held it together until they were in the vehicle and headed down the dark street. She closed her eyes and leaned back against the headrest. Her heart wouldn't slow its frantic pace. Her skin felt hot and flushed. How had she for even a second thought she could do this? She had lost her mind. There was no question about that.

"Tomorrow we'll walk through the house and the woods where you and your sister were found."

Dana's eyes flew open. The heart that had pounded furiously all evening seemed to stutter to a stop. "I'm not sure I'm ready for that." The words were out of her mouth before she could stop them. She was here. She had to be ready.

"That's why we're here, isn't it?" Spence echoed her thought as he braked for the turn into the motel parking lot. "To help you remember."

She couldn't look at him. He was right. That was what she'd gone to the Colby Agency looking for. Someone to help her find the truth.

How did she explain…without giving away her worst fear?

"It's just…harder than I thought it would be." Why was she fighting this? She needed the truth. Her life would never be her own until she knew what really happened all those years ago. She was twenty-nine years old. If she wasn't strong enough to do it now, she never would be. Feeling sorry for herself and being a coward wouldn't get the job done.

When he'd put the car in Park and turned to her, he said, "But that's why I'm here. My job is to make sure we find the facts and that you're fully protected every step of the way."

She couldn't tell him that the one thing she was afraid of most was…herself.

Outside her motel room, he hesitated. "So we're in agreement. Tomorrow we'll visit the house and the woods where you and Donna went that night."

"Agreed." Her throat felt dry. She could do it. She had to do it.

"Then we'll track down Lorie Hamilton and ask the questions that should have been asked of her sixteen years ago."

With a vague nod, Dana unlocked her door and stepped into her room. Her eyes squeezed shut; she closed the door behind her and leaned against it. His suggestions were good ones—made perfect sense.

Then why wasn't she relieved?

Dana forced her eyes open and exhaled a shaky breath. She should just tell him about her nightmares and be done with it. Leaving that aspect, real or imagined, out was undermining what she'd hired him to do.

But would he look for the truth—really look—if he thought she was the…killer?

Her gaze settled on the bed. She blinked, looked again. Terror lit in her veins.

One of the pillows had been pulled from beneath the bedspread and now sat in the middle of the bed. The ends had been scrunched as if someone had held it in both hands and used it to…

…hold over someone's face.

SPENCE UNBUTTONED his shirt and dragged it off his shoulders. His client clearly couldn't make up her mind about what she wanted. For a woman who implied she wanted answers, she sure as hell wasn't acting that way.

What was she afraid of?

He understood she had been traumatized that night in the woods by her sister's murder and whatever happened before and after the fatal act. Was she afraid of the murderer's identity? Was it someone she knew? A parent? A friend? Or neighbor?

Spence had watched kids twist the facts and fabricate explanations to rationalize the horrific. Whether it was a self-protective mechanism or a way to protect others, a wall went up and nothing but those twisted facts and fabrications got past. The only way to get to the truth was to untwist those facts and peel away the layers of fabrications.

Sounded easy. But it wasn't. Even with an adult, like Dana, if the trauma occurred as a child, the decision to set aside the horror in her mind had already been made. That aspect of her past was still cloaked in childlike emotion.

Essentially he was looking for a missing child, her inner child. The one who'd gone into hiding from a reality too traumatizing.

A light rap on the door to his room drew his attention back to the present. Had Dana decided she needed to talk after all? Or did she have something to add to tomorrow's proposed agenda. She hadn't appeared too keen on his suggestions.

He opened the door and found a stranger standing on the other side of the threshold.

Female. Blond hair, green eyes. Late twenties, early thirties maybe.

"Mr. Spencer?"

He glanced left to see if anyone was waiting in the minivan she'd parked a few slots down from his door. That she'd chosen to park away from his room told him she didn't want anyone to know who she was here to see. Her strategy was somewhat pointless since Spence and Dana were the only two guests at the motel. And his car was the only one in the lot besides hers.

"You've got him." Might as well see what this was about. If he was really lucky, the reactions had already begun. The domino effect was the one quick and sure way to get information.

The woman glanced around. "I need to speak with you privately."

Spence stepped back, opened the door wide. "Come on in, Ms.…? I didn't get your name."

The lady ignored his prompt. She stepped inside and waited until the door was closed before meeting his gaze once more.

"There's no one else here, right?"

Spence glanced around. Opted to reach for his shirt and pull it back on. "That's right."

She looked him straight in the eyes then. "You should tell her to go back to Chicago. The only thing she's going to do is make everyone have to relive that tragedy all over again. It's taken years for the people in this community to put—" she drew in a deep breath "—that behind us. We don't need anyone resurrecting those bad memories."

"I would think," Spence said carefully, "that you and the rest of the community would like to see whoever was responsible for those murders brought to justice. I'd say it's long overdue."

The woman just shook her head. "You don't understand," she said, her tone vehement. "She *knows* who killed them. She took that knowledge with her when she left, and we've learned to live with it. Coming back now, after all these years, is not doing anyone any good. It's done. Hurting people isn't going to change the fact that those girls are... dead."

"You have me at quite the disadvantage. Why don't we start over?" The lady was definitely not a fan of Dana's or of reopening the case. He extended his hand. "I'm William Spencer and you are?"

She glanced at his hand, looked taken aback. "I don't see how that's relevant. I just came here to warn

you that you can't trust what she says. She isn't...
right. She never really was, but after the murders she
really lost it. There are things your investigation will
resurrect that will serve no other purpose than hurting
people all over again."

"I take it you're not a friend of Dana's." He
dropped his hand to his side.

Anger blazed across the lady's cheeks. "You ask
her," his visitor urged. "Ask her why she really came
back after all this time." She moved her head side to
side. "She isn't back here for us or even her sister.
She's come back to hurt everyone all over again.
She's still holding a grudge. She's a freak. She was a
freak as a kid and she's still one now. If you can't see
that then you're blind."

Well that was rather blunt and to the point.

When the lady was about to reach for the door, he
asked, "Do you know how many of Donna's old
friends still live in Brighton? I was hoping to talk to
some of them, specifically Lorie Hamilton."

The audible hitch in her respiration told him he'd
hit a nerve.

"Why would you want to talk to...her?"

Just as Spence suspected. His visitor was either
Lorie Hamilton or a close friend of the lady's. "I
have some questions as to her relationship with the
victims. I'd like to get some clarification on exactly

what the nature of their relationship was and when she last saw each of the victims."

Shoulders squared, the woman lifted her chin. "It was a mistake. That's what it was."

"The murders?" he countered. "Or Lorie's relationship with the victims?"

"Maybe you're one of those people who can't see the truth until someone's dead. That's what will happen with *her* back here." With a sharp about-face, she wrenched open the door and walked out. He watched her go. Noted her license plate number as she sped out of the parking lot.

When her taillights had faded in the distance, he closed and locked the door.

More questions.

Spence turned to the wall that separated his room from Dana Hall's. Instinct told him she knew more than she was telling, part or all of which might still be waiting on the other side of that mental wall she'd erected.

But what he'd just learned, that he definitely hadn't known before, was that she had herself at least one serious enemy in her old hometown.

Usually the only surviving victim of a tragedy was looked upon with sympathy.

Evidently not in this case.

What had Dana Hall done that would stick with a person for the better part of two decades?

…can't see the truth until someone's dead.

His gut clenched. He'd never been the one who couldn't see. Was he so determined not to let down his client that he wasn't really seeing what was right in front of him?

Until he knew that answer, they weren't going to get very far in their investigation.

It was time Dana Hall started talking.

Chapter Six

Dana couldn't move.

She stared at the pillow. Waited for the pounding on the door to come. For someone to show up and to say out loud that *she* was the killer. That she had done this awful thing.

Do something!

She pushed away from the door. Walked slowly toward the bed. Her heart thundered, sending sharp pains deep into her chest. She couldn't breathe.

One foot in front of the other. She stalled at the side of the bed, reached out with her right hand and touched the pillow. She shuddered. Images piled one on top of the other in her mind. Feeling the pillow against her face…struggling to breathe. Twisting her body, flailing her arms and legs.

Suddenly the pillow was no longer covering her face. *Die! Just die!*

The final image from her nightmares froze on her retinas.

It was her…she was clasping the pillow against her chest and her sister was lying dead on the ground.

Dana's knees gave way. She crumpled to the floor. Her body shook with the sobs building inside her.

She had killed her sister. She must have killed the others, too.

"No," she moaned. She couldn't have done that. Why would she do that?

Stop. Don't believe it. *Just dreams.* They can't be true. They're not real. *Not* real.

Dana scrubbed at her face with the heels of her hands. Fury rushed along her limbs, searing away the weaker emotions. She couldn't keep doing this. She had to know the truth.

Damn it!

Pushing to her feet, she shoved the hair back from her face and grabbed hold of her courage. Someone was playing games with her.

But who?

And why?

She'd been gone for sixteen years. Her chest squeezed. If she was responsible for…what happened, why hadn't someone spoken up? Why would anyone do this now? She stared at the pillow lying on her bed.

Did someone else know what really happened and

was afraid to tell? Or was someone hiding something that proved Dana wasn't responsible…that she hadn't killed her own sister?

But why would she keep seeing that scenario in her nightmares?

She reached for the door, wrenched it open. Someone had been in her room. She surveyed the parking lot, empty except for Spence's car. The door had been locked when she'd returned from the Bellomy's. How had they gotten in? Had the motel manager given out a spare key? Did he suspect her, too?

Her jaw clenched with fury, Dana stormed out of her room and toward the office. She didn't know who was running the place now since Spence had taken care of getting the rooms. If that pillow was someone's sick idea of a joke, she wasn't laughing.

The office was dark. She didn't care. Dana pounded her fist on the door once, twice, three times. Each time her fury expanded.

A light switched on inside. The blinds on the door parted and narrowed eyes peered out at her from behind wire-rimmed glasses. Some of her anger deflated.

This was crazy. She had to be crazy. Her reactions were over the top. Irrational. Even she recognized she wasn't thinking reasonably.

The door jerked inward. "What's all the racket about?"

The man looked vaguely familiar. Gray hair. Glasses. Tall, thin frame.

"Someone was in my room," she blurted.

His brow furrowed. "What? Your room was broken into?"

She shook her head, then nodded, told herself to calm. "I don't know. But someone was definitely in my room."

He moved back enough to open the door wider. "Come on in here."

Don't act like a frightened child. Dana stepped into the office.

The man shuffled over to the registration desk. Put the long wooden structure between them as if he needed a shield from the crazy lady who'd invaded his office. "Now." He adjusted his glasses. "Tell me exactly what happened."

Take a breath. Speak calmly. "Someone was in my room while I was out to dinner tonight."

"You in twelve?"

Dana nodded.

He checked the room boxes in the hutch behind his desk. "Second key's right here." He turned back to Dana. "Unless you gave someone your key or there are signs of breaking and entering, no one has been in your room but you."

"I'm telling you," she restated as calmly as possible, "someone was in my room." She couldn't tell him about the pillow…he would think she'd taken complete leave of her senses.

He heaved a sigh. "Is something missing from your room?"

She hadn't really looked, but she didn't think so. She said as much.

"Then how do you know someone was in there?"

Dana moistened her lips. "Because things were moved."

The old man's gaze narrowed again. "I know you," he said. "You're Bob Hall's girl. The one…"

His words trailed off, but he didn't have to say the rest. She knew. *The one who didn't get murdered.*

"I'd like a different room." She couldn't sleep in that room. No matter what this man, a man she still didn't recognize, said, someone had been in her room.

He reached for the key to room thirteen. "You don't remember me, do you?"

"Sorry." She shook her head. "I don't." She'd been a kid when her family moved away.

"I'm Samuel Henagar. I was the janitor at the K-8 school until about five years ago when I retired."

Memories of the man pushing the mop and bucket in the school corridors flickered. He never spoke… always watched. Sherry and Joanna whispered about him. Donna, too. They called him a pervert.

"Of course," she finally had the presence of mind to say. "I remember."

"I remember your sister and her friends." He seemed to stare right through Dana. "It's a real shame what happened."

Dana took a step back toward the door. "Thank you for the new room."

"Just turn in the other key when you're finished moving."

Dana didn't turn her back until she was outside the door. He watched her every step of the way. Her heart had started pounding again.

She turned in the direction of her room and bumped into a broad chest. A high-pitched squeak escaped her throat before she could clamp her mouth shut.

"What was that all about?"

Spence.

She sucked in a breath. "I decided to get a different room."

He raised a skeptical eyebrow. "I heard."

How long had he been standing out here listening? "I…my things were moved." She'd meant to add that it happened while they were at dinner, but her brain just wasn't cooperating.

"You think someone was in your room."

Not a question. He'd clearly overheard her discussion with the motel manager. More images from school…from Mr. Henagar flashed through her weary mind. He'd come into the girls' bathroom once… she'd been terrified. He'd insisted that he was only cleaning and that he'd called out to warn anyone in the restroom that he was coming in. But she hadn't heard him.

She crossed her arms and nodded. "Someone was in my room."

"Why didn't you come tell me?"

She should have…but then she would have had to explain things she didn't want to explain just yet. Coward!

"I didn't think." That much was true. She walked around him and headed to her room.

"I have a feeling," he said as he followed close behind her, "that there are things you're keeping to yourself that might be useful to this investigation. I hope that's not the case. Being completely open with me is extremely important to success."

Dana paused outside room twelve. She wrestled with the emotions churning inside her, gained enough of the upper hand to school her expression. When she was certain she could speak in a steady voice, she turned to him. "I hired your agency to help me, not analyze me. I've been analyzed, Mr. Spencer. I don't need your accusations."

He leaned against the doorjamb, studied her at length. She worked hard at not trembling beneath that dark, assessing gaze.

"A friend of yours stopped by a few minutes ago."

She felt her eyes widen before she could stop the reaction. "What friend?" Her pulse started that race toward some unseen goal. Could the person who stopped by be the same one who came into her room? He'd said a friend…but she didn't have any friends in Brighton. Not anymore. Maybe she never had.

"Blonde, green eyes."

Dana's respiration quickened. "Lorie." Had to be. She was the only green-eyed blonde in Brighton. The only one Dana had ever known. She didn't bother explaining again that Lorie and the others weren't really her friends.

Spence shrugged. "She didn't give me her name, but when I mentioned that I was looking for Lorie Hamilton, she reacted. That she was the first name that came to your mind with such a vague description, I'd say my hunch was right."

But how could Lorie have gotten into her room? Why would she do such a thing? "What did she want?"

Spence inclined his head toward her door. "Let's continue this conversation inside."

Dana hadn't moved the pillow…didn't matter. He was here to help her. Only she would understand what it meant lying there. Besides, he was on her side…for now. She opened the door she hadn't bothered locking. Before she could step inside, he held up a hand for her to wait. He went inside first. She held her breath and followed.

Spence looked around her room. Checked all the places she hadn't even thought of, like the closet, under the bed, the bathroom and its narrow window.

"Your window wasn't locked."

Dana eased into the cramped bathroom, trying not to crowd him. He demonstrated by opening the small window over the toilet. Not the raise-up-and-down kind, this one opened in, like a small door.

"Slip a credit card or nail file between the sash and frame, push upward and voilà. The latch releases."

"There's no lock?" How could that meet current safety codes? But it was so small. Could a person actually squeeze through it?

"It wouldn't open so easily except that the latch is worn." He surveyed the window again. "Broad shoulders like mine wouldn't fit through that space." His gaze locked on hers. "But someone small, maybe female, wouldn't have any trouble."

"You think it was Lorie?" Why would she do such a thing? They hadn't seen or spoken to each other in sixteen years! Was she the one who'd called? Obviously she knew Dana was in town.

One wide shoulder lifted then fell. "Do you have reason to believe she would take this sort of measure?"

Dana wanted to say no, but how else could she explain the phone call, the visit to Spence…and the pillow? "I don't know. I can't…there's no reason I know of." She looked straight into his eyes. "But maybe that's what I want to believe."

"You said things in your room were moved." He closed the window and tinkered a moment with the latch. "What was moved?"

"One of the pillows."

He looked puzzled.

"I'll show you." *He's on your side.* She repeated that mantra, gathering courage.

He followed her to the bed. She gestured to the pillow lying there. "It was like that when I came in." Knowing how ridiculous this sounded, she added, "When I left it was beneath the bedspread like the other one." She pointed to the head of the bed where the matching pillow was neatly tucked beneath the spread.

"You believe someone was leaving you a message."

Again, not a question. Dana nodded. "The official conclusions of the investigation cited that the victims had been suffocated with something like a pillow. Something that left no abrasions or bruises."

Spence picked up the pillow, checked beneath it, looked inside the pillowcase. She hadn't thought to do that. Whoever took the liberty of coming uninvited into her room and moved the pillow could have left a message. But they didn't.

He tossed the pillow back onto the bed, "Come on." He turned to her. "You're staying in my room tonight."

"Wait. I…" She couldn't stay in the same room with him.

"I'll feel better if I can see you."

But if she dreamed…

"I'm not taking no for an answer." He walked across the room and picked up the bag she hadn't bothered to fully unpack yet. "Let's go."

She wanted to say no. To pretend that she would be fine. But the truth was, she hadn't been fine in a very long time.

Chapter Seven

Spence watched Dana sleep in his bed.

She'd tossed and turned for most of the night. Occasionally she moaned and muttered unintelligible words. Whether she knew it or not, today she was going to come clean with him. He'd intended to take things a little slower, but the reaction he'd noted so far to her return wasn't going to permit the necessary time.

Though the Bellomys had been kind, it was clear from their reaction, as well as his unidentified visitor's and the motel manager's, that Dana's reappearance had awakened long-slumbering emotions.

After sixteen years, it was surprising that her former neighbors and acquaintances reacted so strongly. The murders everyone who'd lived here at the time would remember, but this was more than that. This was a surprisingly keen mix of emotions.

Dana's eyes opened. She lay still for a few moments before her gaze sought him. She blinked, then sat up.

"I can be ready in fifteen minutes." She threw the covers back and scooted off the bed. Obviously concluding that he was waiting on her.

"I'm ready whenever you are."

He wasn't going to make small talk with her today. As soon as she was dressed and ready to go, they were headed for her childhood home. Mr. Bellomy had told him that the key could be found beneath the rock on the right side of the front steps. Coffee could be picked up en route. He hadn't noticed any drive-throughs in town, but there was a diner.

As promised, fifteen minutes later Dana was ready to go. The jeans, sweatshirt and sneakers made her look far younger than twenty-nine. Her blond hair was pulled back into a ponytail. She didn't look like the same woman he'd met in Victoria's office just two days ago.

"Coffee?" he asked as he opened the door for her to precede him.

"Coffee would be good."

She sounded a bit more relaxed this morning. Relaxed was good. "Coffee would be very good," he agreed.

Climbing into the car he noticed the manager

watching from the office window. He didn't bother turning away when he realized that Spence was staring back.

Odd man. This was a small town; folks were always curious when a stranger came to town. Especially when the stranger was accompanied by the one survivor of the town's only homicide case—a triple homicide case at that.

If Dana noticed the visual exchange, she didn't mention it.

The weather forecast had called for rain. Spence was glad the rain hadn't shown this morning. The overcast sky made for dreary weather, setting an ominous tone.

At the diner, he shut off the engine and turned to his passenger. "Do you want to go in and have breakfast?"

She surveyed the crowd gathered around the tables beyond the glass storefront and shook her head. "I don't think so."

"Cream or sugar?"

"Black." Her attention remained focused on the diner.

Inside, Spence settled on a stool at the counter.

The two waitresses behind the counter shared a look, then one approached him. "What can I get you this morning?"

He glanced at her name tag. "Good morning, Ginger. Two black coffees to go, please."

She hesitated a moment, then busied herself with preparing his order. The hum of conversation and scrape of stainless silver against stoneware didn't diminish, but he felt the stares of several in the room. Again, not unusual in a small town. He was a stranger.

Ginger set the carryout order on the counter in front of him. "Anything else?"

"That'll do it."

"Two ten."

He placed a five on the counter and reached for the bag.

"You're that fellow who brought Dana Hall back to town, aren't you?"

"That's right."

If the unpleasant set of her mouth was any indication, she was no fan of Dana's, either. For a thirteen-year-old at that time, she seemed to have made a lot of enemies around town.

"What'd she come back here for?" the waitress asked. "Things have been nice and quiet since that girl and her folks left. The way it used to be. We don't need her back here causing trouble."

"We're reopening the investigation into her sister's murder. I'm sure you'll all rest easier when the killer is brought to justice."

The silence that had fallen over the diner with his announcement was deafening.

Ginger's face tightened with what looked very much like fury. "That girl knows what happened to her sister. She was the Devil's own, that girl. If she was smart she would've stayed gone."

"Thank you." Spence picked up the bag and turned to go. The diner's patrons immediately turned their attention back to the business of breakfast. But not one had missed the waitress's candid warning.

Funny, he mused as he walked out the door. The Bellomys hadn't mentioned a word about there having been any trouble with Dana or her sister. Good girls was what Bellomy had called them.

Dana hadn't mentioned anything, either.

Had she blocked all of that ugly history?

The only thing he knew for certain was that most people he'd encountered in Brighton so far didn't want Dana Hall back in town. Not even if her presence would solve a sixteen-year-old triple homicide case.

DANA SIPPED HER COFFEE slowly as Spence drove toward their destination. Her full attention was focused on keeping her anxiety level from escalating. Every block closer to her childhood home tightened the band around her chest. Her throat had closed to the point that a tiny swallow, even of the hot brew, was all she could manage.

Being here. Seeing the streets, the trees, the buildings and houses…made her sick inside. A deep breath was impossible. Every face…every voice reminded her of how much she hated this town.

But she couldn't remember exactly why. She had good memories as a small child, all the way up until a couple of months before her thirteenth birthday. But everything beyond that was obscured. The images her mind conjured were foggy, out of focus. She just couldn't recall many of the details surrounding that time. When she'd tried to discuss that part of the past with her mother, she had insisted it was too painful and changed the subject.

Anger kindled inside Dana. That left her with all these feelings…all these uncertainties for sixteen years. Didn't her mother understand that the past was eating Dana alive?

She snapped the lid back on the cup and deposited it into a cup holder. She tried to slow her increasingly rapid heartbeat. As bad as she wanted it, the caffeine wouldn't help.

Her hands had turned to ice by the time the car rolled to a stop in the driveway of her former home. In the light of day the faded paint was even more apparent. The once pristine white siding was now a dingy gray. The windows wore a coat of filth. Though the grass was neatly trimmed, the shrubs were out of control. The first-floor windows were scarcely visible above the untamed bushes.

Spence got out of the car and came around to her door. When he opened it, she sat, frozen a moment before she managed the strength or courage to climb out. Her legs didn't want to work properly, as if just being here had diminished her coordination. He led the way, as though she were here for the first time. The key was under the rock, as Mr. Bellomy had said.

On the porch, she stood behind Spence as he unlocked and opened the door.

Dana hadn't set foot inside this house in almost sixteen years. A lifetime.

The stale smell hit her nostrils, but it was the underlying scent of home that rammed her senses. Despite the passage of time, she could smell the life she had once lived here.

"Why don't you show me around?"

She nodded, the motion jerky. The front door opened into a small entry hall. The home was a typical center-hall, two-story colonial. To the right was the dining room, to the left was the living room and down the center hall, behind the staircase, was the kitchen.

They wandered through those rooms. The furnishings were draped in white sheets like ghosts from the past. Every glass, cup and spoon had been left behind. Her parents had taken nothing—not even clothes. They'd said it was too hard to look at any of it, much less use it.

The kitchen counter felt cold beneath her fingertips. Images and voices bombarded her mind. Her mother calling them to dinner. Her father simultaneously watching the news and reading the paper.

"Upstairs," Dana said when they made the complete circle and paused at the bottom of the staircase, "are the other bedrooms. My parents' room was the large one at the end of the hall."

"Where's the room you and your sister shared?"

"This way." Dana led him back through the kitchen, to what used to be a garage. When her father had built his two-car detached garage they had turned the one that was part of the house into a large den.

Dana drew up short at the door. A large padlock prevented their entrance.

"Did your father padlock the door?"

Dana started to say no but then changed her mind. "I honestly can't say. Those final weeks here are just a blur. I know I didn't sleep in there after…that night."

"Let's check with Mr. Bellomy."

Dana followed Spence as far as the porch, but she

had no desire to interact with anyone else this morning. She'd seen the way the people in the diner had stared at Spence and then at the car when they'd realized she was in it.

No one wanted her back here.

Particularly, it seemed, Lorie Hamilton.

Dana just couldn't remember why.

When Spence returned he carried a large tool. Like a big set of pliers. "What's that?"

"Bolt cutter."

A frown tugged at Dana's brow. "He didn't have a key?"

"No key."

That anxiety she'd been fighting since waking was revving into high gear. Dana tried to slow her breathing. Tried to talk herself down from the ledge where she was headed—a full-blown panic attack.

Spence positioned the tool and strained to snap the metal ring of the lock. A couple of attempts later, it popped, then fell loose.

"All right." He laid the tool on the floor and wiggled the disabled lock free. He wrapped his fingers around the doorknob and gave it a turn.

Dana's breath stalled in her lungs as he swung the door inward. The room was pitch-black. The windows had apparently been covered. With no electricity, they couldn't turn on the lights.

"Stay right here," Spence said. "I'll get a flash-light."

He didn't have to worry; she wasn't going into that room alone.

Seconds later he was back, flashlight in hand. He clicked on the beam and moved into the room.

Dana's gaze followed the flashlight's beam, settling on the walls. Hideous drawings marred the pastel pink paint…pictures of devils and witches and circles with the slashes across them that meant forbidden or prohibited. Broken pieces of furniture were strewn all over the floor. The room had been ransacked or vandalized…

But it was the writing on one wall that had her reaching for something to hold on to.

Dead and gone to hell.

Chapter Eight

Chicago, Illinois

Ian Michaels slid the list of names across the conference table to Victoria. "I've narrowed down the six names Thomas Casey provided."

Victoria reviewed Ian's conclusions. All lethal enemies of her husband...all capable of most any imaginable or unimaginable crime. "Did Thomas agree with your conclusions?" Thomas Casey was head of Mission Recovery, a shadow operation associated with the CIA. Thomas was Lucas's former director as well as a close friend.

Ian nodded. "He pinpointed four of the six names." Ian gestured to the list. "You'll notice the check marks. Those are where Casey believes the focus should be."

Thomas Casey had also put out feelers to update

intelligence on those listed. Victoria could depend on Thomas. His unit was made up of the most highly trained men and women in the country. As thorough as Thomas and his people would be, Victoria still wanted Ian and Simon on top of this as well. This could just as easily be an enemy of the Colby Agency.

That sickening sensation of dread churned in her stomach. Allowing her granddaughter to attend pre-school under the circumstances was one of the hardest decisions she'd ever had to make. But the child wanted desperately to be with her friends. She loved school. Ian's wife, Nicole Reed-Michaels, was stationed inside the school to keep an eye on Jamie. The faculty and staff at the school were on alert as well. Brad and Elaine Gibson, another of the Colby Agency's husband-and-wife teams, were standing guard on the campus grounds.

Victoria would not attempt to contact Jim and Tasha unless the situation escalated. If contact was even possible. She didn't want to worry them unnecessarily. At this point, the threat to the family was nothing more than an underground rumbling. Still, Victoria had taken every possible precaution. No risk would be left to chance.

She wanted desperately to talk to Lucas. To hear his voice. Reaching him was very nearly an impossible task as well. For the first time since he retired, he had been called in as an advisor and active participant on a brewing situation in the Middle East. The negotiation talks were taking place at an undisclosed location with the strictest government security measures in place. Thomas had assured Victoria that he would get word to Lucas.

Forty-eight hours and still waiting. Victoria's nerves were frayed.

Mildred appeared in the doorway. The relief on her face told Victoria before she uttered a word that she'd come with good news. "Lucas is on line two."

Thank God. "Thank you, Mildred." Victoria selected the speaker option and opened line two. "Lucas." Her throat tightened with emotion and for an instant Victoria couldn't speak. "I'm glad you could call. I have Ian and Simon in the conference room. You're on speaker."

"Are you all right?"

The worry in her husband's voice twisted Victoria's heart. She hated the idea of being so far apart and adding this burden onto his already full plate. "I'm fine. Jamie's well-being is my primary concern right now."

"Casey filled me in. He also mentioned a couple of names, Heddison and Dutton. I would be surprised if either one of those two possessed the courage to resurface considering they're wanted for treason, but you can't be too careful. Casey has two of his specialists tracking down the top six he and Ian discussed. As soon as he knows anything at all, he'll make contact."

It was so good to hear his voice. Just knowing that he was on the case filled Victoria with renewed courage. "I'm sure we'll have this under control very soon." She prayed that would be the case. "Meanwhile, we're looking into every known enemy of the Colby Agency." There were other things she wanted to say to Lucas, but those would have to wait.

"We will get through this," Lucas reiterated. "No one is going to touch my family." The pause that followed punctuated the emotion in his tone. "I'll call you tonight, Victoria."

Warmth filled her chest, chasing away the fear. She had Lucas. She had her extended family here at the agency, as well as Thomas Casey and his specialists. Victoria had every reason to be strong and confident. "Until then," she said in parting.

When the line closed, Victoria reclined in her chair and took her first deep breath of the day. Everything was going to be all right. No one was going to hurt her family ever again. She was far too aware of evil's reach… She'd learned that lesson the hardest way of all when her only child, her son, went missing more than two decades ago. Evil had snatched him at age seven, and she hadn't been able to find him. Jim was missing for nearly twenty years. During that time he was tortured, enslaved…and worse.

She would not allow his child to suffer that same tragedy.

As if fate had deemed that moment the perfect opportunity to counter Victoria's firm vow, Mildred burst into the room.

"Nicole is on line one." Mildred glanced from Victoria to Ian and back. "She says it's urgent."

Fear resurrected in Victoria's heart. Ian put the call on speaker before she had the presence of mind to react.

"What's going on, Nicole?" he asked, an edge in his tone.

Tension seemed to push the very air out of the room.

"We have a fire alarm," Nicole explained, the chatter of excited children and the high-pitched shrill of the alarm in the background. "According to the director this is *not* a drill."

Victoria's heart surged into her throat.

Before she could speak, Nicole went on, "I'm holding Jamie's hand. She's right beside me. We're filing out of the building with her class. Brad and Elaine are searching the grounds for anything or anyone out of place."

Victoria pushed back her chair and stood. "I'm on my way." She could not sit here and wait to see if this was a mere coincidence. She had to be there.

She needed to see with her own eyes that Jamie was safe.

"We'll be there in ten minutes," Ian told his wife before rushing to catch up with Victoria at the door. "Don't worry," he said with a hand on her arm. "No one's getting to Jamie without going through Nicole first. You know that."

Victoria tried to nod, but her muscles simply wouldn't cooperate.

He was right. Anyone after Victoria's granddaughter would have to step over Nicole's dead body to accomplish their goal.

Even knowing that her best agents were on top of the situation, Victoria was terrified.

Chapter Nine

Brighton, Indiana

Chief Gerard and Mr. Bellomy stood in the middle of the defaced room. Spence had pulled loose the plywood covering the windows. The morning sun filled the space, highlighting the ugly images and threatening messages.

From the doorway, Spence watched the two men. Mr. Bellomy was clearly and genuinely stunned. He had not seen this before. According to Gerard, this vandalism had occurred the night after the Halls left Brighton. Gerard had gone through the motions of investigating the malicious act, and then he'd padlocked the room to prevent anyone who might sneak into the house from stumbling upon this ugliness. He'd boarded up the windows, even going so far as to nail the sashes shut. From that time forward, Mr.

Hall had asked his neighbor to keep a close watch on the place.

"So," Spence ventured as the chief moved toward the door, "you concluded that this was nothing more than an act of vandalism."

Gerard didn't make eye contact as he waited for Spence to step aside so that he could exit the room. There was more to this than a random act of mischief.

"The wife and I heard the talk," Bellomy murmured, more to himself than to anyone else, "but we thought it was just foolishness."

"Talk?" Spence looked from Bellomy to Gerard. "There was talk like this?" He jerked his head toward the room.

Bellomy wandered into the hall, apparently wanting to hear the chief's answer as well.

Spence had sequestered Dana to the neighbor's house. Mrs. Bellomy promised to make her hot tea and keep her away from *this*.

"You know how kids are," Gerard protested. "When something terrible happens they liken it to some movie they watched. The Devil. You know."

Who was this guy kidding? "Give me a break, Chief. This goes deeper than that."

Gerard removed his cap and swept a hand over his balding head. "There was an incident or two before the murders."

"What kind of incident?" Spence prompted.

"The month before the…murders," Gerard began, "Patty Shepard's cat went missing. When the child found it, the poor animal had been mutilated and hung by its neck from a tree."

When the chief didn't continue, Spence again prodded, "This relates to the murders how?"

Gerard shrugged. "Mr. and Mrs. Shepard insisted that Patty and Dana had been arguing at school. Evidently Dana thought Patty was making fun of her. Several other students contended that Dana promised to get even."

"You think Dana mutilated the girl's cat?" And the investigation at the time of the murders didn't think that might be relevant? Admittedly, Spence didn't want to believe Dana Hall was capable of such an act, but he couldn't be certain. He'd known her a sum total of seventy-two hours. These people had known her, at the time, her entire life. If there was any chance whatsoever that she was capable of that kind of cruelty, she should have been viewed in a different light during the homicide investigation.

"Dana denied any knowledge of the act," Gerard countered. "Her parents were mortified. There was no history of that kind of behavior." He turned his hands palms up. "Like I said, kids jump to conclusions, overreact. Anyone could have killed that cat.

But because Dana and Patty were on the outs, that's the story that was told."

Spence wasn't dismissing this information so easily. "You said a couple of incidents."

Gerard heaved a sigh. "Mr. Spencer, Dana Hall, like her sister and the other two girls who were murdered, was a good girl. Dana didn't go around killing animals, and she certainly didn't kill anybody."

Spence considered his visit from Lorie Hamilton and the waitress Ginger's comments. He wasn't so sure it was as cut-and-dried as the chief wanted to portray.

"But there was another incident," he pushed.

"Another girl's dog went missing," Gerard confessed. "The animal was never found." He shook his head. "The dog could have run off, been picked up by someone passing through. We don't even know that it was harmed in any way."

"But Dana was somehow tied to the incident," Spence suggested.

"The girl, Ginger Ellis, insisted that Dana threatened to get her for copying one of her papers and claiming the story was hers. Dana received an F on the paper. Her teacher accused her of plagiarism."

Spence couldn't believe what he was hearing. "And no one looked at this as relevant to her sister's murder? Typically sisters jump to each other's rescue. You didn't find it questionable that Dana had these troubles and then her sister and friends end up murdered."

Murder never occurred without motivation.

Never.

All one had to do was find the motivation, then the suspects stacked up like a deck of cards.

Gerard and Bellomy shared another of those secretive looks.

"I should get home and check on Dana," Bellomy announced before pushing past Spence.

When the front door slammed behind Bellomy, Gerard moved in close to Spence.

"Now you listen to me, Mr. Spencer," Gerard stated in warning. "The citizens of Brighton were torn to pieces by those murders. I'm not gonna watch you or anybody else stir that ugliness all over again. I'm telling you, the killer was a stranger. Somebody passing through. You won't find any killers here. Let it go. Dana needs to put the past behind her and focus on the life she's been blessed with."

Spence resisted the urge to shake his head. "You know, Chief, I always thought a man of the law served justice, no matter the cost. Obviously I was wrong."

Gerard's glare bored into Spence's. "You're wrong, all right. Wrong to bring her back here. Folks don't want to look at her. She reminds them too much of the past and the pain they've all fought hard to put behind them."

With that, Gerard walked out.

Spence wandered up the stairs and checked the other rooms. The one Dana and her sister had shared was the only one defaced.

Outside he stood on the porch and surveyed the house across the street. He found it strange that the Bellomys lived right across the street but hadn't been aware of the vandalism. Or that Mr. Hall had asked Mr. Bellomy to look after the place without mentioning what had happened.

Even more unbelievable was the chief's dismissal of the incident. Had he even bothered to investigate the vandalism before sealing off the room?

Probably not. The chief had decided the case would go unsolved when no evidence of a stranger had been collected. Spence doubted he had seriously looked at anyone who knew the victims.

There had to be a reason.

As easy as it would be for Spence to presume the man simply hadn't done his job, he didn't get that kind of vibe from Chief Gerard. This was about covering up the truth. The question was, why?

Dana stepped out onto the porch across the street. Spence studied her movements as she folded her arms over her chest and leaned against the nearest post. Her gaze roved the house that had been her childhood home, eventually landing on him.

The answer to that one pivotal question, as well as several others, waited behind that mental wall she had erected.

He had to find a way around that wall.

Taking into account what he'd just learned, the truth might impact her world in a way she hadn't anticipated before now.

The seemingly perfect life Dana had led as a child was, it seemed, nowhere near perfect.

Spence had to ask himself a couple of hard questions. Was Dana Hall shielding herself from the past because she was a murderer? If he breached that wall, would the memories he unleashed send her over an edge from which she might not be able to return?

He needed expert advice.

That was the thing about the Colby Agency. Victoria employed only the best…from all walks of life.

Dr. Patrick O'Brien didn't practice psychology anymore, but he was one of the agency's top investigators. One call to him and Spence would know exactly where to go from here.

If Dana Hall were lucky, it wouldn't be to a psych ward…or prison.

Chapter Ten

Dana didn't understand any of this. Why would someone do this to her room? To her home? An ache had started behind her forehead, deep in her skull.

Was it possible that someone had hated her and Donna enough to do this and Dana couldn't remember? That seemed impossible.

Did the person responsible for this have anything to do with Donna's death? Or Sherry's? Or Joanna's?

The whole situation got more confusing with every passing hour.

Dana wandered down a step. She watched William Spencer pace back and forth on the porch across the street, his cell phone pressed to his ear. Was he calling to inquire how to handle the case now that other issues had come to light?

None of it made sense.

She descended the final step and walked slowly along the sidewalk until she reached the street.

Mr. and Mrs. Bellomy had wanted her to stay, not to go back across the street. But Dana couldn't pretend anymore that she could ignore the past. She had to find the truth—whatever it was.

Then she would deal with the consequences.

This morning…seeing the horrible images and words someone had scrawled across her bedroom walls, Dana understood that she couldn't be a coward anymore. It was past time to do this and do it right.

Her sister and her friends deserved to have their killer brought to justice.

No matter who the killer was.

Her cell phone vibrated. She jumped. *Calm down.* It was probably her mother again. If she kept avoiding her calls, she would definitely show up here. Dana slid two fingers into the pocket of her jeans and tugged out her cell phone.

Deep breath. Just do it. "Hello."

"Dana, what're you doing?"

Her mother. "Mom, I'm doing what I should have done years ago."

"I'm on the verge of rushing to Brighton and bringing you home. You don't—"

"Mom." Dana took a moment, reminded herself that this was her mother and no matter how furious and frustrated she was, she had to remember that this was an act of love. "No matter what you do, I'm going to finish this. So just stop. I'm a grown woman. I don't need your permission to do what I know in my heart I have to do."

There were a lot of questions she could ask her mother, but that would only make bad matters worse. Her mother would refuse to discuss any of it. The less ammunition she gave her mother, the better.

The back and forth went on for a minute or two more before her mother gave up. Dana slid her phone back into her pocket.

The words on the wall of her old bedroom flashed in front of her eyes. She had to know what happened.

She had to.

Her gaze settled on William Spencer as he ended his call. He tucked the cell phone into his pocket and looked her way.

As they stood there, looking at each other from opposite sides of the street, she realized it was time. Everything about the past grew more confusing with each new discovery. She felt helpless and almost hopeless with the lack of understanding as to how it all tied together. Chief Gerard was no help at all.

If she felt that way, Spence had to be completely baffled. It was time she trusted someone with her nightmare scenario. Maybe it was a mistake. But it was a risk she was going to have to take.

He hadn't walked away yet, and that was a lot more than she could say about anyone else in her life the past decade or so. Her "weirdness," as they called it, usually sent people, particularly men, running.

Spence couldn't help her if she didn't cooperate.

She needed this to end…one way or another.

DANA MOVED DOWN THE STEPS of the Bellomy's house, then headed in Spence's direction.

He'd expected to have to go over there and basically drag her back over here. Not that he could blame her. Whatever had happened sixteen years ago, it had been personal and extremely twisted. No matter how the chief wanted to ignore what was right in front of his eyes, there was a major cover-up going on here.

And it started with Dana Hall.

O'Brien had suggested that Spence go for a firm tone, building the momentum until he felt compelled to let up. There was no way to know how far Spence could go until he'd begun. It was definitely time to get started.

"I guess," Dana said as she climbed the steps to her childhood home, "I freaked out a little."

Understandable. "Seeing your room defaced in

such a manner would freak out most anyone." She appeared calmer now, maybe even a little determined. Her shoulders were square, her gaze fully engaging his.

"You said you wanted to go to the place…" She glanced away. "Where they found…us."

A major step in the right direction. "I believe that could be useful in helping you remember."

"This way."

Dana led the way behind the house and into the woods. The air was heavy with humidity, but not as bad as yesterday. The path through the woods was a little overgrown but unmistakable. The sun filtered through the trees, lighting their journey.

Spence could easily picture two thirteen-year-olds traipsing through the dark woods, blond hair flowing in the breeze. Had someone followed them that night? The woods stretched along the road on either side of the Hall home. The killer could have parked most anywhere and made his way to this path or directly to the stream from another route.

Spence heard the trickling of water well before the path opened into a clearing on the bank of the wide stream. Boulders were scattered about. Good for seating. It didn't appear anyone had been here recently. There were no signs of a campfire or litter of any sort.

Was this place off-limits as Dana's bedroom had

been all these years? The chief couldn't exactly put a padlock on the woods. But something had kept the curious from venturing here.

Then he saw the reason.

Crosses and angels. Clusters of what appeared to have been dried flowers and…was that garlic cloves? The primitive, weatherworn items hung from dozens of branches. He'd been so focused on the stream and the surrounding ground area that he hadn't looked up at first.

Dana turned all the way around, taking in the bizarre decorations.

"Does any of this mean anything specific to you?" he asked, grasping at straws. "Was any of it here… before?"

She shook her head. "There was nothing like this here…before." Her gaze collided with his. "I suppose it has something to do with the pictures drawn on the bedroom walls."

No doubt. "Why don't we sit?" He gestured to a couple of boulders. "Relax a minute, then we can go over what you remember from that night."

Dana couldn't block the trembling she felt inside. She worked hard not to let it show. Courage, strength…she needed both right now.

Deep breath. Another. Then another. Okay. Just get it over with.

"We lay right there." She gestured to the patch of grass near the stream. "You could see the stars from there." That was about the only spot where the tree branches didn't touch. She shivered when she surveyed the hanging crosses and angels. Who would do this?

"You talked about driver's licenses and—" Spence shrugged "—girl stuff."

Dana nodded. "We always felt safe here. It was our place. Only our closest friends came here with us."

"Like Joanna and Sherry."

"Yes."

"Tell me about Ginger Ellis."

"Same grade as us. She made the cheerleading squad that year." When Donna didn't, she left off. Dana closed her eyes and banished the memory of how upset Donna had been.

"She accused you of being responsible for her missing dog."

Dana tried to summon the memory, but it wouldn't come. "I remember there was talk about it, but my parents kept me home from school for a few days after that. Donna came home upset. She'd gotten into a fight with some of Ginger's friends. Taking up for me, I suppose." Her sister had always taken up for Dana. Maybe because she was two minutes older. Being older, even if only by minutes, Donna had felt like the big sister.

"What about Patty Shepard? Do you recall the incident involving her cat? That was around the same time."

That she remembered all too well. "Patty accused me of trying to start a fight with her over something she'd said."

"What did she say?"

Dana met his eyes then. Her stomach clenched. "She said I was weird. You know, a freak or something."

"You didn't confront her about it?"

Dana shook her head resolutely. "I wasn't the confrontational type. I never got into fights or arguments. I didn't have to. No one seemed interested in bothering me. The rest of the kids pretty much left me alone until…right before the murders."

Spence didn't ask any more questions for a while. He seemed to mull over what she'd told him. Dana twisted her fingers together. If she could just slow the pounding in her chest. She knew how this all sounded. Like she was pretending nothing ever happened. But it was true. Until Patty Shepard and Ginger Ellis started those rumors, Dana had always been invisible. Or it had felt that way. Her sister was the one who made all the friends. She was the popular one. Not Dana.

"Just a few more questions."

Dana searched his face, tried to read some hint of the conclusions he'd reached. Impossible. "All right."

"You and your sister were twins. Identical twins."

"Yes."

"Did anyone ever get the two of you confused?"

Dana started to say no. Donna was the outgoing one. Miss Popular. She had a million friends. Dana was quiet. The bookworm. Though their physical features had been mirror images, their personalities were polar opposites. No one ever mixed them up…except once.

"Donna hated math class. She was certain she would fail seventh-grade math, so I took the class for her while she covered my English class."

"No one ever suspected?"

"Not to my knowledge."

"Could Donna have pretended to be you in other situations?"

Dana frowned. "Why would she do that?"

"You were accused of having problems with the Shepard girl and the Ellis girl. Is it possible Donna was the one who had trouble with them while pretending to be you?"

"Patty was a grade higher and Ginger…" Dana wanted to deny the possibility. To say that her sister wouldn't have been involved with either girl, but that wasn't true. Patty was a second-year cheerleader;

The Harlequin Reader Service—Here's how it works: Accepting your 2 free books and 2 free mystery gifts places you under no obligation to buy anything. You may keep the books and gifts and return the shipping statement marked "cancel". If you do not cancel, about a month later we'll send you 6 additional books and bill you just $4.24 each for the regular-print edition or $4.74 each for the larger-print edition in the U.S. or $4.99 each for the regular-print edition or $5.49 each for the larger-print edition in Canada. That's a savings of at least 15% off the cover price. It's quite a bargain! Shipping and handling is just 50¢ per book. * You may cancel at any time, but if you choose to continue, every month we'll send you 6 more books, which you may either purchase at the discount price or return to us and cancel your subscription.

* Terms and prices subject to change without notice. Prices do not include applicable taxes. Sales tax applicable in N.Y. Canadian residents will be charged applicable provincial taxes and GST. Offer not valid in Quebec. All orders subject to approval. Books received may not be as shown. Credit or debit balances in a customer's account(s) may be offset by any other outstanding balance owed by or to the customer. Please allow 4 to 6 weeks for delivery. Offer available while quantities last.

▼ If offer card is missing write to: Harlequin Reader Service, P.O. Box 1867, Buffalo, NY 14240-1867 or visit: www.ReaderService.com

NO POSTAGE
NECESSARY
IF MAILED
IN THE
UNITED STATES

BUSINESS REPLY MAIL
FIRST-CLASS MAIL   PERMIT NO. 717   BUFFALO, NY

POSTAGE WILL BE PAID BY ADDRESSEE

HARLEQUIN READER SERVICE
PO BOX 1867
BUFFALO NY 14240-9952

Send For
2 FREE BOOKS
Today!

I accept your offer!

Please send me two free *Harlequin Intrigue®* novels and two mystery gifts (gifts worth about $10). I understand that these books are completely free—even the shipping and handling will be paid—and I am under no obligation to purchase anything, ever, as explained on the back of this card.

❏ I prefer the regular-print edition
382 HDL EYK3   182 HDL EYQR

❏ I prefer the larger-print edition
399 HDL EYLF   199 HDL EYQ3

Please Print

| |
| FIRST NAME |

| |
| LAST NAME |

| |
| ADDRESS |

| | |
| APT.# | CITY |

| | |
| STATE/PROV. | ZIP/POSTAL CODE |

Visit us online at
www.ReaderService.com

Offer limited to one per household and not valid to current subscribers of *Harlequin Intrigue®* books.

Your Privacy — Harlequin Books is committed to protecting your privacy. Our Privacy Policy is available online at www.eHarlequin.com or upon request from the Harlequin Reader Service. From time to time we make our list of customers available to reputable third parties who may have a product or service of interest to you. If you would prefer for us not to share your name and address, please check here ❏.

▲ Detach card and mail today. No stamp needed. ▲

H-I-07/09

Ginger had just made the team. Both had been in Dana and Donna's gym class. Still, her sister was loved by all. She never had trouble…unless she was taking up for Dana. "I suppose it's possible." That was as far as she was willing to go along those lines. Why would her sister have gone so far? She would never have hurt an animal.

Whispers from the past echoed in Dana's ears as if refuting her conclusion. Dana shook off the creepy sensations.

Dana understood what he was getting at. It was time she told him the truth. She was the one he needed to be looking at as a suspect.

"There's something I haven't told you." Her pulse jumped. She'd taken the first step. There was no turning back now.

"Take your time," he said quietly. "And remember, I'm on your side."

But how long would that last when she told him about her dreams?

"When the nightmares started they were a little vague. Just unnerving."

"That's fairly typical after a life-altering trauma."

"Then the images became clearer and clearer."

Dana moistened her lips and tried to take a breath, couldn't manage it. Don't stop now. Tell him. Just tell him.

"I dream that I'm lying on the blanket with my sister and I fall asleep. Like I told you. Then..." The point of no return. "Then suddenly I'm holding a pillow...over my sister's face and she's trying to get away, but she can't." She swallowed back the threatening emotions. "Because I'm sitting astride her. I have her arms pinned down with my knees...it..."

Those images flashed through her mind then, as if to confirm her words. She shook with the force of it. Dear God. How could she have killed her own sister? How could...?

Dana couldn't hold back anymore; she broke down. The sobs just kept coming, kept rocking through her.

A strong arm was suddenly around her. Spence consoled her with quiet words, kept that arm tight around her trembling shoulders.

When she could speak again, Dana scrubbed at her face and turned to him. "What if I killed my sister? And the others? How could I have done such a thing?" She dropped her face into her hands. "I don't understand."

"Sometimes dreams distort what really happened. The fact that you survived and your sister didn't has heaped a lot of guilt onto your shoulders. You may be seeing yourself as the killer merely because you survived."

Dana wiped her eyes and nose and tried to calm the hiccupping sobs. When she'd regained her composure again, she admitted, "I've never considered that possibility." Tears burned her eyes again. "I just always assumed I could be guilty." She closed her eyes and clung to hope. "I was so afraid. But I have to know for certain."

"And you will."

Dana looked up at him. "How can you be so sure?"

"Because I'm not going to stop until I know what really happened here. The chief isn't being on the up and up with us. The whole investigation feels like a cover-up was going on. I just don't know who he's protecting."

"Maybe it's me." Her voice quavered.

"Maybe," Spence admitted. "But that's what we're going to find out."

She'd expected him to want nothing else to do with her when he learned the part she'd kept to herself. Why was he taking it so calmly?

"But what if I killed her?"

Spence pushed the hair from her cheek with the tips of his fingers. "I'm a decent judge of people, Dana. I knew you were hiding something, but I don't think you're a killer."

She started to argue, but he stopped her with a touch of his forefinger to her lips.

"Don't keep obsessing on that one aspect or you'll ignore everything else. Explore your memories, let your dreams flow unimpeded. You might see more than you've allowed yourself to see until now. We have to consider the big picture. There are people we need to talk to. Like Lorie Hamilton, Patty Shepard and Ginger Ellis. I'd like to interview Joanna's and Sherry's parents as well."

That was not going to be easy. The possibility of any of those people cooperating was little to none.

But they had to try. He was reasonably sure that Ginger Ellis was the waitress he'd met at the diner. Ginger wasn't a common name and this was a small town.

"Let's go." He stood, gave her a hand getting up. "We're going to that diner and we'll have lunch. Then we'll start with Lorie Hamilton."

If they could find her.

The thought of going to the diner and having people stare at her wasn't exactly palatable. But she had Spence on her side.

She wasn't alone.

The walk back through the woods was filled with a sense of relief rather than the anxiety she'd felt on the way in. Having finally admitted her deepest fear had removed a tremendous weight from her chest.

It was the first time she'd trusted anyone enough to tell them the truth.

They'd just rounded the corner of her childhood home when Spence stalled.

Dana started to ask him what was wrong, but then her gaze lit on the car.

The windshield was smashed. The two tires within her line of sight were deflated. But it was the words painted along the side of the dark-blue sedan that shook her to the core of her being.

No more victims.

Chapter Eleven

Spence stood by while the chief and one of his deputies wrote up the report on his vandalized car. Fury lashed through him each time he considered Gerard's nonchalance about the situation.

Like I told you, son, folks around here aren't too keen on Dana digging around in a past they've worked so hard to forget.

Son. Spence gritted his teeth. The condescension he could overlook, but the cavalier attitude about the murder of three young girls Spence couldn't abide.

The man wasn't interested in the truth, that much was crystal clear.

And it made no sense.

Dana sat on the front steps of her house. She looked lost and afraid.

Alone.

Again, there was that question. What had she done

that was so terrible her former friends and neighbors didn't want her back in town?

And what was he doing letting this get so far under his skin? Not getting personally involved was the first rule of any investigation. He knew better.

"Well." The chief strolled over to where Spence waited. "That's about all we can do for now." He tucked his notepad into his shirt pocket. "Since the Bellomys didn't see anything and no evidence appears to have been left behind, 'cept maybe some prints that we can run for the good it'll do us, I'm not sure we'll be able to nail down the perp. But we'll do all we can."

Spence was certain he would. "I have every confidence, Chief." Every confidence that this would be just like the triple-homicide case in his jurisdiction. Whatever this man's motive for overlooking the criminal activities of the good citizens of his town, Spence had a feeling it had more to do with hiding some secret than with being inept.

"You folks need a ride back to the motel?"

Spence shook his head. "I have a rental car headed this way as we speak."

"All right then." The chief glanced at Dana. "If you need anything else you can let me know."

So he could do nothing? Spence didn't think he'd bother. "Thanks."

Chief Gerard turned his back and started toward his patrol car on the street, but then he hesitated. He turned back to Spence. "Take my advice, son. There are no answers to find here. Take that girl home before the real trouble starts. I can't control how folks feel."

Spence wasn't about to justify the comment with a response. He let the chief walk away. After he'd climbed into the patrol car with his deputy and drove away, Spence joined Dana on the steps.

For a long moment she sat staring at his damaged car. Spence considered what he should say in hopes of making her feel less responsible, but he wasn't sure that was possible. She now fully believed that she was the reason for every bad thing that had happened in her hometown.

Realistically, he recognized that she might, in part, be correct. But some part of him, a part deep inside, wouldn't let him write her off just yet.

But then, he'd always championed the underdog.

"Everyone can't be wrong," she said quietly, as if she'd read his mind. "It has to be me."

"If it were that simple," Spence offered, "someone wouldn't be trying so hard to send us packing."

She met his gaze. "What do you mean?"

Spence surveyed the street where Dana Hall had lived for the first thirteen years of her life. "When a person or a group wants someone gone as bad as they clearly want you out of here, there's a reason."

"Maybe they're afraid," she said. Her breath hitched with the anxiety no doubt pulsing inside her. She indicated the vandalized car. "'No more victims.' That pretty much says it all."

Her shoulders shook. Spence couldn't help himself. He put his arm around her and pulled her against his shoulder. He knew better. But she was all alone. He was the only one representing her rights.

Was that a mistake?

Was she a killer?

He didn't think so.

Spence looked down at her and hoped like hell he wasn't allowing his need to protect override his professional logic.

The tow truck and rental car arrived. Spence took care of the paperwork and watched as his car was towed away. He opened the front passenger door of the car. "Come on," he said to Dana. "We have people to see."

The uncertainty in her eyes tugged at his senses. Made him want to put his arms around her and promise her he would fix this. He would find the truth and make everything right.

But that was a promise he couldn't make.

The only thing he could do was find the truth.

For better or worse.

LORIE HAMILTON HAD MARRIED her high school sweetheart and settled right here in Brighton. Her name was now Lorie Venable. She was a stay-at-home mom with two children and one dog, a ranch-style home and a minivan. Finding her was easy, since he'd noted her license plate number when she'd visited him at the motel. One call to the Colby Agency and he'd had her name and address.

Spence parked his rented car at the curb. He turned to Dana. "Stay calm, and let me ask the questions," he reminded her.

Dana nodded.

She looked terrified. Her hands shook, but her expression told him she was determined to do what she could.

The slats of the blinds on the front window parted briefly as Spence and Dana moved up the sidewalk toward the neat front porch belonging to Lorie Venable.

Spence hoped the woman inside wouldn't call the chief. He wasn't ready to be run out of town just yet. The chief's warnings had grown stronger and stronger with each meeting. He wasn't going to be happy when he learned the investigation was continuing.

Raising his fist to knock, Spence was surprised when the door opened.

"What do you want?" Lorie glared from Spence to Dana then back.

"We have a few questions, Ms. Venable. Five minutes is all we need."

Lorie glanced back quickly as if ensuring no one, probably her kids, were in earshot. "I've said all I have to say."

Beside him, Dana shifted but she held damn steady beneath the woman's bitter glare.

"You said," Spence said, not about to give up so easily, "that Dana knew what happened. What is it you believe she knows?"

Lorie's eyes widened, and her expression turned to one of disbelief. She pulled the door closed behind her. "I'm not going to talk in front of her!"

"Ms. Venable, you can—"

"Why?" Dana cut him off. "Why can't you talk in front of me? I can't remember what happened that night," she pressed. "I want to remember. I need to know. If you can help me, I'm begging you, please help me."

A new blast of rage obliterated the disbelief cluttering Lorie's face. "Are you insane? You know what happened," she accused. "Stop acting like you don't. The only reason this case is still listed as unsolved is because the chief knows the killer. He's just not saying to protect what's left of *your* family."

"What're you talking about?" Dana demanded. "How could letting a killer get away be protecting my family? My sister is dead! My father is dead because of what happened."

Spence clasped the fingers of his right hand around Dana's arm as a signal that she needed to calm down. He hoped she would get the message.

"I don't know what your daddy had on the chief back then," Lorie roared right back, "but he didn't do his job. Your sister is dead because *you* killed her. The only person who's in denial is you!"

Dana staggered back a step. Spence tightened his grip on her arm. "Ms. Venable," he said calmly, hoping to staunch the rocketing tension, "you can't be certain who killed Donna Hall and her friends. If you were so certain, wouldn't you have gone to the press by now? After all, if the chief didn't do his job, what kept you from calling the state police or the FBI? Unless, of course, there's some reason you don't want to get involved beyond throwing around accusations."

The red of rage drained from the woman's face. Her hand clasped the doorknob as if she were considering taking refuge inside.

"Please," Dana urged, her voice breaking, "help me. If I…did this…I just want the truth."

Lorie moved her head side to side in disgust. "How can you play this game? You know what you did. You tortured all of us. You mutilated Patty's cat! Don't pretend you don't remember." Lorie shifted her renewed fury to Spence. "If you contact me again in any way, I'm calling the chief. I don't want her near me or my family."

Lorie Venable went back inside her house and slammed the door.

Dana started to shake. Spence steadied her as they made their way back to the car. When he'd gotten her settled in the passenger seat, he rounded the hood and slid behind the wheel.

When he'd started the engine, Dana said, "I don't understand what she's talking about." She leaned heavily into the seat. "I vaguely remember there was trouble about a cat. My sister kept telling me to ignore all of it. That they were just picking on me."

Spence took his foot off the brake and set the car in motion. "Do you have any school yearbooks? Maybe one from the year before you moved away?"

Dana thought about that for a moment. "I think so."

"Would you have taken mementos like that with you when you moved?" If so, they'd have to try to obtain one from the school. Spence wasn't going to hope for cooperation.

"No. We didn't take anything from the house except the clothes on our backs and one family photo album. Mom didn't want the reminders around. She and Dad left everything at the house here exactly as it was."

Dana fell silent. Spence didn't have to wonder what she was thinking. The house remained exactly as it had been, except for hers and Donna's room.

"We need that yearbook," he stated frankly. The images from her time in school might just prompt others. It was worth a shot.

A glimmer of courage showing, Dana affirmed, "I think I can find it."

THE YEARBOOK HAD BEEN TUCKED away in a cedar chest along with other precious mementos from their childhood. Dolls, baby shoes…all the things that remind a mother and father of their children's early years.

Spence had felt concern when Dana first began to pick through the items. But she held up well enough. She didn't linger on any one item, instead she focused on finding the yearbook.

He'd stopped at a convenience store and picked up refreshments. Now, back at the motel, they thumbed through the yearbook.

He wanted her to relax and let the emotions and memories flow. No pressure. No expectations. Most of all, no fear.

"Sherry and Joanna." Dana pointed to a snapshot

in a collage of others. "And, of course, that's Donna. They were always together."

Spence had seen a professional photo of Donna in Chief Gerard's case file, but this was different. This one was real life, all smiles and not posed.

"Why weren't you in the photo?" It was his understanding that Dana had been a part of her sister's group.

"They were at a ball game. I never went to any of the sporting events."

The introvert. "Your sister was the outgoing one."

Dana nodded. "She liked being in the middle of things, being popular. Loved the attention, I guess. Not me."

Spence studied the lady sitting next to him on the bed. Her profile was delicate and classically attractive. What had banished Dana Hall into herself?

"What about at home? Did Donna like being the center of attention there as well?"

Dana considered the question a moment, then said, "I don't think it was a conscious effort. She was just the one who talked the most. She discussed current events with our father. Always wanted to help our mother plan birthdays and holiday get-togethers. I was just sort of in the background."

Invisible. She didn't have to say it. He understood that place. He'd seen it in others. Typically the child most abused was the one who required the least. And also very typical was Dana's need to blame herself for all the bad that happened.

Spence reminded himself that he was giving the lady a whole hell of a lot of credit. He couldn't be one hundred percent positive that she wasn't responsible in some capacity for one or all of these murders.

But he wasn't ready to go there just yet.

"What did your sister's friends think of her trying out for the cheerleading squad?" The three, Joanna, Sherry and Donna, appeared fairly inseparable. Were her friends happy to sit on the sidelines and cheer her on as her sister had?

"Oh, no, they all tried out." Dana touched the faces in the photo and smiled. "Like the three musketeers. They did everything together."

Was that also why they died within a week of each other? A shot in the dark, yet one worth considering.

"Joanna and Sherry didn't make the squad, either?"

"Not technically. I think they might have been alternates like Donna." She shrugged. "Something like that. Mostly I remember they were depressed for days."

"When Lorie hung out with your sister, did she hang out with Joanna and Sherry, too?"

Deep concentration lined its way across Dana's smooth brow. "I can't remember ever seeing all of them together, but," she said as she turned her palms up, "that may be something else I've forgotten."

"Okay." He closed the yearbook and placed it on the bedside table. "Next we go to the library and look at what the newspapers were printing at the time of the murders. You may see something that jars your memory."

The yearbook hadn't stirred anything significant. But maybe the headlines would. According to O'Brien it could be a single word, person, image or event that might suddenly tap through the wall into that well of hidden recollection.

After that, Spence had other people on his list to interview. Like Patty Shepard and Ginger Ellis. Maybe he would start with Ginger, the outspoken waitress, since she appeared to have plenty to say.

Dana crossed the room to where her purse sat on the table. "You know I forgot to turn in one of my keys to the manager. He may try to charge you for three rooms."

It wasn't like the motel had any other guests, but Spence understood what she meant.

"We can turn in the key to room thirteen." He reached for his car keys. "You leave your stuff in twelve, but you'll be sleeping here."

Dana's lips parted as if she might argue that decision.

"No arguments. I don't want you out of my sight for the rest of our time here."

She sighed. "Okay." She laughed, but the sound held no humor. "According to everyone else, it's me you should be afraid of."

Spence gave her a reassuring smile. "I'm reserving judgment for now."

Dana hung the strap of her purse on her shoulder and lifted her gaze to his for an extended moment. "Thank you."

"For what?" He drew his eyebrows together in question. "For not being afraid to share a room with you or for doing my job?"

"For reserving judgment."

She opened the door and stepped out; he followed. He inserted the key in the lock and gave it a turn. The way things were going around here, if someone wanted in the room a mere lock wouldn't stop them. But Spence wasn't going to make it easy.

Dana's hand settled on his arm. When he looked up she sent a look toward the street.

A Brighton Police Department cruiser was parked in the supermarket lot across the street.

Spence could guess what that meant. Lorie Venable had reported their visit.

The chief would be watching their every move from this point forward.

Odd. Dana wanted the truth. Nothing more.

Shouldn't the chief of police want that, too?

Chapter Twelve

Dana felt cold.

Ice cold.

Her vision blurred as she stared at the screen.

Tragedy Strikes Small Town a Second Time

…a third girl is found dead…

Dana couldn't read this stuff anymore. She'd lost count of the newspapers. The dozens of headlines churned in her brain. It was like reading a story about someone else. She knew it happened, yet she couldn't recall experiencing any of it personally.

What was wrong with her?

Why couldn't she just remember that night!

Dana closed her eyes and tried to stop the spinning inside her head.

"Hey," Spence said quietly.

For one moment Dana kept her eyes closed, enjoying the feel of his warm hand on hers. He made her feel safe. No one had made her feel this protected since…before that night. It didn't hurt that he was tall and strong-looking with broad shoulders. She liked his eyes. Dark and soothing.

"They're ready to lock up. They're just waiting for us to go."

Dana opened her eyes and looked around. He was right. The library was deserted save for the two women behind the front desk. The return counter and carts had been cleared. She'd had no idea it was eight o'clock already.

"Right." As she grabbed her purse she felt compelled to apologize. "I'm sorry we've wasted more time."

"Anything we do that gives us more information is not a waste of time."

She had to try and remember that. Finding the answers, the truth, was the goal. Each detail discovered was one additional, however tiny, step toward that seemingly elusive goal.

Going to the Colby Agency was the best decision she'd made in a long time. No, scratch that. It was the best decision she'd ever made. The idea of facing these people—people she'd known her whole life—alone was unimaginable. He made it bearable.

Spence was right beside her as they passed the front desk. With him next to her she could tolerate the way the librarians stared at her. She knew what they were thinking. What everyone in this town appeared to think. She couldn't let that deter her from her goal.

As she reached for the door, a poster snagged her attention. She stalled, read the words that accompanied the image of an author's upcoming release.

Private Confessions...One Woman's Journal Journal.

She'd kept a journal when she was a kid.

Images and words exploded in her brain.

"Is something wrong?"

Dana blinked. She turned to Spence. "I kept a journal."

The anticipation that lit his eyes signaled that he understood this could be important.

It could be really important.

Dana couldn't get to the car fast enough. Her mind whirled with the possible places she might have hidden her journal. She'd kept one, faithfully. She just had to recall where she'd put it last.

In her room somewhere.

The room was trashed. What if someone had found it and taken it?

Dana couldn't catch her breath until they were in the car and headed toward the house on Waverly Street. She'd written her innermost thoughts in a journal since she could form sentences. How had she forgotten that?

Her heart was racing now. Her palms were sweating. Would she have written about that night?

"Hurry."

"Well," Spence said, "since that deputy is still following us around, staying under the speed limit might be the best course of action."

Dana hadn't realized she'd said the word out loud. "Sorry, I was just thinking aloud."

Spence flashed her a smile. Even with nothing more than the dash lights, the gesture made her feel secure. And unafraid.

Ice-cold fear stabbed deep into her chest.

What if they were right?

What if she was the one…?

He would hate her then.

When Spence parked in the driveway, Dana couldn't move.

He climbed out of the car.

She couldn't breathe.

He hesitated at the front of the car. She could see him in the moonlight.

Move. Her body refused to cooperate.

He walked around to her side of the car and opened the door. "Come on," he urged gently. "I'll be right there with you every step of the way."

She could do this. She *had* to do this.

Her fear about this was so tangible…so over-whelming. She felt like a helpless child.

Dana put one foot on the pavement and pushed up and out of the car. She could do it.

The house was dark. Even the moonlight didn't help the looming structure. Her movements were stiff as she followed Spence onto the porch. This had been her home as a child. The only home she'd ever known. She shouldn't be afraid. Nothing bad had happened inside this house…until after she moved away.

Spence unlocked the door. "Wait. I should get a flashlight."

He jogged down the steps and hurried across the street. The lights were on at the Bellomy house. It wasn't ten yet, so they were probably still up.

Dana hugged herself. She looked around the dark porch and tried to picture playing here. The porch had been her mother's favorite place to sit in the evening. She and Dana's dad would wave to the Bellomys, sip their evening tea and talk about how things were changing in town.

How was it she could remember those details and not one thing she and Donna had done on those same evenings? It was like her entire personal history began and ended that one night. Nothing before was clear, nothing for days afterward that could be re-trieved.

The night's chill had leached deep beneath her skin by the time Spence returned with a heavy-duty flashlight. Inside, he waited for her to catch up. She'd stalled in the doorway.

"You want to wait until morning to do this?"

It took every ounce of courage she possessed not to take him up on that suggestion. Waiting until tomorrow would only delay what she'd already waited sixteen years to know.

"No. I'm through waiting."

"Where would you like to start?"

He had to know the answer to that question. There was only one place to look.

Her bedroom.

"The bedroom. You go first," she urged.

He moved down the hall, allowing the flash-light's beam to rove the area in front of them. Dana's pulse wouldn't slow. No matter how long she held her breath or how deep the breaths, her heart rate wouldn't slow.

At the door, she braced for the cruel images beyond. He opened the door, and she followed him into the room. The ugliness rammed her senses all over again. Voices whispered in her ears.

You can't go…they don't want you there.

Dana shivered.

It's not my fault. They just don't like you.

Dana resisted the impulse to put her hands over her ears. It was Donna's voice, but she didn't remember her saying those things.

"You okay?"

Dana jerked from the disturbing thoughts. "Yes. I'm fine."

"Why don't you hold the light? I'll pick through things."

She accepted the flashlight and took a deep, steadying breath. She could do this. Focusing the beam on his movements, she mentally inventoried the items as he sifted through the strewn pieces of her past.

A blue-and-white school sweater. The teddy bear she hadn't been able to give up as a preschooler. Donna's favorite teen magazine. Stuff…so much stuff.

"Did you have a special hiding place for your journal?" he asked after digging around for what felt like an hour.

"I must have." Why couldn't she remember? Damn it!

Think! It couldn't be that difficult. How many places were there to hide things?

They opened each drawer, sifted through the closets…

Nothing.

Her anxiety gave way to frustration. She'd kept a journal. It had to be here.

She needed it to be here so this could finally be over.

While she held the light, Spence disassembled the beds. Nothing under the mattresses.

Nothing anywhere.

Okay. Think. Maybe she'd hidden it somewhere else in the house. If her goal was to keep her private thoughts a secret from her sister, their shared bedroom wouldn't have been the best hiding place.

"We should check the other rooms," she suggested. She hoped with all her heart this wasn't going to be another dead end.

"Wait."

Spence held her back when she would have headed for the door. "What's wrong?"

"Do you smell that?"

Dana inhaled a lungful of air. There was an odor… it tingled in her throat.

"Smoke."

The single word he uttered settled like shackles around her limbs. She couldn't move. Couldn't speak.

The flashlight fell from her limp fingers. Bounced on the floor, sending bobs of light across the wall.

He grabbed her arm and reached for the abandoned flashlight simultaneously. "We have to get out of here."

Smoke…the word filtered through the layers of disbelief. That meant…

Fire.

Chapter Thirteen

It was past midnight.

Dana sat on the steps of the Bellomy porch and watched the firemen roll up their hoses.

The full moon seemed to spotlight the blackened shell that had once been her home. All their worldly possessions had gone up in flames. Going through the rubble might reveal a few salvageable items.

The things from before her life as she knew it ended.

"Dear, are you sure I can't get you something?"

Mrs. Bellomy hovered nearby. She wanted to help. She'd offered a blanket, a cup of hot chocolate, a good, stiff drink. But Dana felt too numb to interact with another human on any level.

Knowing she was waiting for some sort of response, Dana managed a faint shake of her head. Thankfully that seemed to satisfy Mrs. Bellomy. She disappeared back into her home.

Spence and the chief were still deep into what looked like a heated exchange. The spotlights the firemen had settled around the house to facilitate their efforts showcased the tension between the two men.

If Dana's memories about the journal could be trusted, then that insight into the past was lost. All her sister's things. Their stuffed animals and dolls…the artwork their mother had collected over the years.

Everything.

Gone.

Her sister and father were dead. The family home was destroyed. If something happened to Dana's mother, there would be no one left who remembered the time when they were happy.

Dana tried hard to recall that time. Before the murders. Way before. But those memories were foggy. When had she stopped remembering those days?

Was there something wrong with her? Really, truly wrong. Like a brain tumor? There had to be a logical explanation of why she couldn't recall those final days of her sister's life. Was her condition growing progressively worse? How else would she explain the fogginess that appeared determined to descend over all she should be able to recall?

The screen door behind Dana squeaked as it

opened, then closed with a swat of wood against wood. Mrs. Bellomy settled onto the steps next to Dana.

Dana closed her eyes and tried to summon some kind of emotion. She felt utterly blank. She couldn't cry. Couldn't scream. Nothing.

"I'll call your mother in the morning, if you'd like. No use upsetting her in the middle of the night."

Dana hadn't even thought of that. Of course her mother would need to know. "Thank you."

"Carlton tried to properly see after the place all these years. But it's not the same when no one's living in a home. Things just go down. It's like the house is sad because it's empty and it slowly, surely falls apart."

Dana's gaze followed the organized chaos across the street as the firemen continued to go about the final steps of their business. Mrs. Bellomy was right. The house had been abandoned…left to disintegrate.

"The chief says it was probably a faulty electrical problem."

Dana nodded, the words scarcely registering.

"I know you feel you have to do the right thing, Dana," Mrs. Bellomy went on, "but I don't think you're doing yourself any good here. Carlton and I were so happy to see you again, but this is tearing you apart. Why don't you put all this behind you and get back to your real life in Chicago? You can't do any good here. Nothing's going to change no matter what you find."

For the first time since Dana had decided to go to the Colby Agency, she seriously questioned the whole point of what she was doing.

Mrs. Bellomy was probably right—they all were.

Dana was hurting people, particularly her mother, by being back here. No one would cooperate with her efforts. She hit a brick wall everywhere she turned. And the few details she did discover all pointed to what her nightmares already told her.

She had killed her sister...

Why was she bothering to look?

Was the chief protecting her? Had her mother and father been protecting her when they rushed her away from here?

If her nightmares were true, then Dana deserved nothing better than what she'd had the past sixteen years. She'd muddled her way through college, hadn't had a real relationship. She barely dated. She existed...nothing more.

She didn't even deserve that.

The numbness faded, leaving an emptiness that was far worse.

She should have died that night. Not Donna. Everyone had loved Donna. Dana had been nobody. Her life had never impacted anyone's until sixteen years ago when she'd destroyed three families, including her own.

"You're right." Dana pushed to her feet. "I should go."

Mrs. Bellomy called after Dana, but she just kept walking. Spence and the chief were still deeply involved in their conversation. No one noticed as she passed. Dana was glad. She didn't want to talk anymore. She didn't want to think.

And she definitely didn't want to remember.

Walking in the direction of town wasn't a conscious decision. It was just the way the road went, and she followed it.

As bright as the moon was, there were no stars visible. The glow filtered through the barren trees. Leaves danced along the pavement as the wind picked up. Dana shivered.

A car had rolled up next to her without her noticing. She started. The driver slowed, peered out at her and then drove on. Dana hugged her arms around herself. She looked around the tree-lined street that led into Brighton proper. It was a few more blocks before she reached the next neighborhood. She probably shouldn't have taken off on her own since she obviously had no friends around here. So far everyone she'd encountered wanted her out of here and considered her crazy or a killer or both.

The sound of another car approaching sent adrenaline searing through her limbs, initiating the fight-or-flight response. The headlights cut across her and pierced the darkness in front of her. She kept walking. Didn't look back.

By the time the vehicle was next to her, she was certain her heart was going to burst from her chest. She refused to look. Kept her attention straight ahead.

The sound of a power window lowering hummed in her ears.

"Dana, what're you doing?"

Spence.

Thank God.

He braked hard. "Get in the car."

She started to say no. But what was the point?

What was she doing?

The tears came from nowhere. Flooded her vision then streamed down her cheeks. She tried to pull herself together, to be strong. But that wasn't happening.

A door slammed. Footsteps echoed on the pavement. And then she was in Spence's arms.

He held her tighter than anyone had in a very long time.

Dana sagged against his chest. She cried so hard that her whole body shuddered with the effort.

She was so lost.

What did she do now?

What did it even matter?

SPENCE WATCHED DANA SLEEP. She'd cried for a solid hour. There had been nothing he could do but hold her. Nothing he could say except to make the same promise. He would find the truth.

He crossed the room, pushed back the generic drapes and peered out at the night. A deputy's cruiser sat in the parking lot across the street. Chief Gerard had made it clear that he wasn't tolerating any more trouble out of Spence or Dana.

If Spence or Dana went anywhere near Joanna Cassidy's parents, legal action would be taken. Since Sherry Sanford's family had moved to Denver, they were beyond the chief's jurisdiction. However, he warned Spence that he had already called the Sanfords and urged them not to take calls from Spence or Dana.

A stalemate.

The chief was fighting him every step of the way. Why?

And this whole business about the fire being related to the home's incoming electrical supply was ludicrous. The exterior service panels were in the off position, had been for nearly sixteen years. It was true that the meter was still in place and that the electrical service was still active to the service panel, but the fire had started on an exterior wall beneath that service panel. A service panel that was *off*.

Spence was no master electrician, so he couldn't say for certain that the chief's suggestion was impossible. When considered with the vandalism to the first-floor bedroom in the house as well as his car and the reaction of a number of citizens to Dana's presence, foul play should be suspected.

And investigated.

That wasn't going to happen because the chief wanted Spence and Dana out of here today. An arson investigation would only give them reasonable cause to prolong their stay in Brighton.

Spence had already considered consulting Victoria about bringing the FBI into this. There was a major cover up going on here, and Spence wasn't at all sure he could handle this alone.

He knew how the law worked, no question.

Without tangible physical evidence, he didn't have a leg to stand on. All he had was an overwhelming gut instinct that the chief was hiding the truth.

How could anyone not see that?

Had the parents of the victims been so devastated that they couldn't dredge up the wherewithal to induce the chief to do his job?

Were the citizens of this town so convinced that Dana was guilty that they refused to see anything else?

Evidently.

Spence closed the drapes, checked the lock on the door and sat down on the bed. He needed sleep. Later today they had only one avenue available. Attempt to interview Patty Shepard and Ginger Ellis. The chief hadn't cautioned him to stay away from those two in particular.

If that didn't give him something more to go on, he would have no choice but to call Victoria.

Spence didn't want to fail the Colby Agency.

But more than that, he didn't want to fail Dana.

As if his thoughts had summoned her, her eyes opened. She blinked, stared at him a moment, likely mentally replaying the night's events, then pressed her hand to her mouth.

"We're going to start early," he said, in an effort to give her hope. "We'll go to Ginger Ellis first, then to Patty Shepard. We're not giving up." *Not yet.*

She rolled onto her back, swiped at her eyes. "My entire life I've been the one who didn't bother anyone, didn't speak out of turn. I was always quiet and obedient. How can this be real?" Her gaze met and held his. "How could I have killed three people and not remember? How could all these people believe I'm pure evil?"

Spence traced a tear she'd missed that trickled down her cheek. "There are a lot of unanswered questions. And we're not settling on a conclusion until we have the answers. When we have the truth, we'll deal with it. Whatever it is."

"But how?" She squeezed her eyes shut and shook her head. "How am I supposed to deal with it?"

"*We* will deal with it," he reiterated. "You don't have to do anything alone."

He had sworn he would never again get personally involved on this level. And here he was, involved all the way to his heart. But he couldn't let her do this alone. No way.

He kept seeing that little thirteen-year-old girl all alone in the woods with her sister's body. The invisible little girl that everyone made fun of and blamed any and all trouble on.

The throwaway kid.

There were far too many in this world.

Even sixteen years later, as an adult, Dana Hall was still treated as utterly dispensable.

She blinked back the renewed shine of tears, swiped at her nose. "After all you've been told, why would you want to help me? I know you're a smart guy, but it seems like a dumb decision."

He laughed softly. "I guess I've always been a sucker for the underdog."

Their gazes held as emotions stirred hotter, deeper inside him. He couldn't leave her to the wolves…he had to stand up for her. No matter that she appeared weak and confused. He could only imagine the strength it took to continue living with this burden day in and day out. It would have been so much easier to end all the pain and guilt. The way her father had. But she'd stood strong and waited for the day that her courage was solid enough to come back here and find the truth.

As weepy and confused and uncertain as she seemed, the determination and bravery required to come this far made him ache to know more of her.

To heal that injured woman so long neglected.

A faint smile trembled across her lips. "You know, the last time a man looked at me like that he kissed me. But that was a long, long time ago."

Anticipation had him leaning closer. "Then you're way overdue."

He lowered his lips until they touched hers. Her breath caught at the rush of sensations. His heart thumped hard. He'd never wanted to kiss any woman as much as he wanted to kiss Dana.

It was forbidden, unprofessional.

It was dangerous, if half of what he'd been told was true.

It was the only way he would survive this moment.

He pressed his mouth firmly over hers and kissed her the way a man should kiss a woman. With utter respect and tenderness and mind-blowing desire.

She made the sweetest sound. Her fingers threaded into his hair and pulled him closer still.

The kiss went on and on. Deeper and deeper, then slower and sweeter.

He would have given most anything to make love to her. But she was vulnerable right now. He wouldn't take advantage of that. Instead, he lay down beside her and held her close. Let her feel how much he wanted her. Let her know that he was there for her.

Whatever the cost, he was in for the duration.

Chapter Fourteen

Chicago, Illinois

Half past two. Victoria stood at the door of the guest room where Jamie slept so peacefully. She'd scarcely made it through the afternoon briefing. Spence had checked in. Things were moving slowly in Brighton. Victoria would simply have to leave the worries of the day-to-day operations up to Mildred and Simon. She had to focus solely on protecting Jamie.

The school hadn't been able to explain the fire alarm. But Nicole, Elaine and Brad had ensured Jamie's safety during the ordeal.

They had no leads. Nothing. It was as if this threat had come from thin air. And yet, it was there, expanding with each passing moment.

Victoria's heart ached with the pressure and fatigue of the past seventy-two hours. She wished

Lucas were home. She questioned her decision not to attempt to reach Jim and Tasha at least a dozen times a day.

Victoria closed her eyes. *Please, God, protect this child. Let them do what they will to me, but please, please, keep this child safe.*

For the first time in her life, Victoria wondered if she could do this. She'd had to be strong for so long. She was tired. Tired of…

No. She squared her shoulders and lifted her chin in defiance of her own emotions. She was blessed in many ways. She had no right to feel sorry for herself. Weakness was not allowed.

She would keep her grandchild safe while she tracked down these bastards. And then she would make sure they never threatened her family again.

Or she would die trying.

Chapter Fifteen

At 7:30 a.m. Ginger Ellis wasn't at the diner. According to her coworker, she was scheduled to come in from eight to three, but she'd called in sick. The coworker had also pointed out that Ginger's last name was Larson now.

A quick check of the local telephone book had given Dana her address. Ginger had married high-school football hero Derek Larson.

The photos in her school yearbook, which was the only item from her past Dana now possessed, had reminded her who Derek Larson was. Why didn't photos of Lorie or Sherry or Joanna help her remember more?

Dana stared at the modest brick home down the street from where Spence had parked. Ginger shared

the home with her husband. She had a real life, a relationship. Dana wasn't sure she would ever have
those things.

"You ready?" Spence asked.

Dana held her breath, braced to say yes, but a
large yellow school bus pulled to the curb in front of
Ginger's house. "Wait." She watched as Ginger
waved to a small boy dashing toward the waiting
doors of the bus.

Ginger apparently had a child, too.

Envy stirred in Dana's heart. She didn't mean to
be envious, but she couldn't help herself. All she
needed was the truth…then maybe she could move
on and have those things.

Spence got out of the car and came around to
Dana's side. She opened the door and joined him.

She could do this. It was the only way. Chief
Gerard just wasn't cooperating in any capacity. Dana
needed answers. Someone had to start telling her
more than what a bad person she'd been. That part
was clear, even if Dana had no memory of executing
all those heinous deeds.

Strange. Why wouldn't she remember incidents
that happened well before her sister's murder?

She glanced left then right. No sign of any official
vehicles. Spence had spent twenty minutes losing
the deputy assigned to watch their every move.

Chief Gerard wouldn't be happy.

Too bad. Dana had a right to know what happened sixteen years ago.

That could very well be where her rights ended.

She shivered.

"You're sure you're up to this?"

It was nice having someone worry about her. She'd lived alone and on her own for so long. Not allowing anyone close had taken its toll. Maintaining a meager, too-busy-to-visit relationship with her only remaining relative, her mother, hadn't been easy either. But it was for the best. Her mother refused to talk about Donna's death. She refused to discuss their life in Brighton at all. Small doses of contact were necessary.

In answer to Spence's question, she nodded. "This is our only option." They were quickly running out of leads to follow.

Before they'd taken another step toward the Larson home, the front door opened. Ginger hurried out, her purse draped over her shoulder. Dana's nerves jangled. Ginger climbed into her SUV and backed out of the drive. Thankfully headed in the opposite direction from where they'd parked.

Dana's relief was short-lived. Now they wouldn't be able to talk to her. Every step forward and they got shoved back three.

"Get back in the car."

The stern order startled her into action. She hustled back to the car.

"We're going to follow her?" Dana dragged her seat belt over her lap.

"We're going to do," he said as he eased away from the curb, "whatever is necessary."

Emotion crowded into Dana's throat. He was going above and beyond for her. She'd heard the Colby Agency was the best in the business. Now she could see why.

She'd waited a long time for someone with the courage to help her see this through.

Whatever the truth turned out to be, she was ready to face it.

GINGER ELLIS LARSON DROVE to a community park on the west side of Brighton. Spence pulled to the side of the street half a block away.

"What is she doing?" Dana leaned forward to watch the woman walk toward the center of the park.

Another woman waved and Ginger veered in that direction. "She's meeting someone. See the lady at the swings."

"That's…" Dana unsnapped her seat belt and moved forward a few more inches. "That's Lorie Hamilton—I mean Venable."

Lorie hugged Ginger before giving one of the swings another push. A small blond girl squealed with glee as she swayed back and forth.

"It's possible this could be a coincidence. A weekly activity between two old school buddies," Spence suggested, but his instincts weren't buying it.

"Look." Dana pointed to another woman striding toward Ginger and Lorie. "That's Patty Shepard or whatever."

This got better and better. They could interview all three at the same time. The chief wouldn't be happy, especially since he'd warned Spence to stay away from Lorie. But this was a public park. A dozen or so mothers and twice that many kids were scattered about.

While Spence and Dana watched, Lorie plucked the little girl, presumably her daughter, from the swing and the three women moved to a sandbox where other children played. Lorie settled the child there then ushered her friends to a bench a few feet away.

"They're talking about me, aren't they?" Dana's gaze collided with his. The fear that had been notably missing this morning was back.

"Probably." He placed his hand on hers and gave it a squeeze. "But that just makes our job easier."

Dana chewed her lower lip and shifted her attention back to the three ladies in question.

"We'll watch a couple of minutes, then we'll join the party." The chief would be called, but Spence could get in a number of questions in the seven or eight minutes it would take the man to get here.

Those two minutes ticked by like an eternity. Dana remained on the edge of her seat as if she could somehow hear the discussion if she watched closely enough.

Ginger was the demonstrative one. She used a lot of body language. Lorie paced, splitting her attention between the discussion and her daughter in the sandbox. Patty was the still one. Her arms were hugged around her waist. Her ankles crossed.

"Okay." Spence pulled the keys from the ignition. "Let's crash this tea party."

Spence kept to the sidewalk in hopes of not attracting attention until they were closer to the threesome. Dana stayed close behind him. He'd gotten within twenty feet of the bench when Ginger noticed his approach.

"Good morning, ladies."

Patty and Ginger were on their feet instantly. Lorie looked torn between running for her daughter and standing her ground with the others.

Dana fell back a step when the women's attention shifted to her.

"I was hoping to speak to each of you," Spence

announced as he took a position well within conversation range. "It must be my lucky day to catch all three of you together."

Lorie lifted her hands, waved them back and forth. "Chief Gerard already warned you not to bother me." If the panic in her eyes was any indication, she was figuratively caught in the act.

"Not to worry." Spence held up his hands in stop-sign fashion to negate her response. "We're not here to cause trouble. We just have a few questions that any or all of you should be happy to answer."

Ginger glared at Spence. "I'm not answering anything." She turned that fierce glare on Dana. "You shouldn't have come back here."

Patty looked more terrified than panicked or angry. She was the weak link. Thirty seconds and Spence had already learned an important detail.

"I don't know why you keep saying that," Dana countered, her words directed at Ginger. "I grew up here, went to school with all of you. Why won't you help me? I need to know what happened."

"They're dead," Lorie blurted. "What do you hope to accomplish stirring all this up again?"

Dana hugged her arms around her waist. "Because I need to know." She gestured to the sandbox where the little girl played. "You went on with your lives. Have husbands. Children." She shook her head. "I couldn't do that. Because I can't stop trying to remember what happened. I can't...live with this any longer. Don't you understand that?"

Ginger went toe-to-toe with Dana. "You killed your own sister. You don't deserve to have a life."

Before Spence could push between the two women, Patty made the move. "That's enough." She stared a long moment at Ginger. The fear was gone, replaced by something like fury. "No one knows for sure what happened. We weren't there." She turned to Dana. "If you were guilty, you would've been arrested."

"How can you say that?" Lorie demanded. "Look what she did to FeFe!"

Patty's face turned grim. "That was a long time ago. This isn't about that."

"It is," Ginger argued, "if she's psycho."

"My question," Spence cut in now that emotion had overridden logic, "is, why weren't any of you questioned about the murder of Donna Hall?"

Three startled gazes collided with his. Ginger was the one who spoke first, "What's that supposed to mean?"

Spence turned his palms up. "You," he said to Patty, "believe Dana mutilated your cat." He shifted to Ginger. "You said she was responsible for your missing dog." His gaze settled on Lorie then. "You were head cheerleader, and you're convinced she killed the two alternates for your squad. Seems to me," he concluded, "that all three of you had motive for wanting to get even. Maybe you killed the wrong sister. Dana and Donna were identical twins after all. It was dark. You could have mistaken Donna for Dana."

Silence seemed to echo across the park. As if everyone gathered in the long, green space had paused to hear the women's response.

"Is that why you're meeting this morning? To make sure you have your stories straight?"

Ginger and Lorie started talking at once. Each adamantly denying his ridiculous theory. Patty just stared at him, her face pale with disbelief.

"One of you," Spence interrupted the chaos, "or maybe all of you, knows something. Don't think this is going away. I won't stop digging until I know exactly what happened. So, if you're hiding anything, I would come clean soon. Trust me, if I can't find the answers I'm looking for, I will take this to the FBI, the way Gerard should have done sixteen years ago."

Before either of the three could speak, Spence added, "You know where to find us." He touched Dana's elbow and gestured toward the car. "Let's go."

Not one of the three said a word as Spence and Dana walked away.

That was good. The exact reaction he'd wanted. Now they would seethe and worry. One would break. His money was on Patty.

Chapter Sixteen

Dana's mind was still reeling with the clash of emotions in the park when the blue lights appeared in the rearview mirror.

"That took longer than I'd expected," Spence commented as he pulled his rented car to the side of the street. He turned to Dana. His dark gaze settled on hers. "Don't worry about this. There's only so much he can do. Just stay calm, and don't let him get to you."

Dana nodded her understanding. She tried to slow her breathing, to calm her racing heart but that wasn't happening with Chief Gerard striding toward the driver's side of the car.

Not once in her life had she gotten into trouble with those in authority. She'd been accused of trouble as a kid back in school, but it had never amounted to anything more than talk. Even after Donna's murder, she had been treated as a victim…not as a criminal.

That was no longer the case.

For years Dana had suffered with the nightmares…with the questions and fears that she was responsible for her sister's death. But for the first time in all those years she realized that, as Spence said, something was very, very wrong with the way the investigation of her sister's murder had been conducted.

Chief Gerard was hiding something or covering for someone.

Maybe it was *her*.

Maybe it wasn't.

Either way, she needed to know the truth.

Spence powered his window down. "Good morning, Chief."

"Mr. Spencer." Gerard pushed the brim of his hat up his forehead. "I'll need you and Miss Hall to follow me down to the station house."

"Are we under arrest?" Spence asked bluntly.

The chief scratched the forehead he'd bared. "I guess that depends on whether or not the three of my citizens you keep harassing wish to press charges."

Dana bit her lip to hold back a gasp. Surely he wouldn't arrest them. This was insane. She'd been treated like a monster since she got here. Her family home had been vandalized and burned to the ground. She was still the victim and no one seemed to get it.

Spence acquiesced with a nod. "We'll be right behind you, Chief."

Gerard stalked back to his cruiser, climbed in and whipped back onto the street. He was not a happy camper. Dana wrung her hands. She'd taken two weeks' vacation from work. Maybe she was going to need a lot longer.

"He'll growl, make a fuss," Spence said, drawing her attention back to him. "But we haven't crossed the line yet. We'll be fine."

For the first time in a long time, Dana wasn't afraid. She trusted Spence. He knew what he was doing. Most important, he was on her side.

AT THE POLICE STATION, Dana held her head high as she and Spence followed the chief down the long corridor to his office.

Chief Gerard paused before reaching his office. He turned back to Spence. "We're going to need a statement from each of you." Gerard reached for the door to his right. "Mr. Spencer, if you'll have a seat in here." The chief gestured toward the end of the corridor. "Miss Hall, you can follow me to my office."

What was this? That old, too familiar fear trickled into her veins.

"Miss Hall is my client," Spence challenged. "We'll give our statements together."

"This is my town, sir, and we'll do things my way here."

Dana stepped forward. "That's fine." She glanced at Spence. "I'll be okay."

"Of course you will," Gerard assured her. "This is just a formality."

Dana didn't give Spence time to argue. She walked directly to the chief's office. She wasn't afraid of what he might say. She was way past that. This had gone on too long…way too long.

She settled into the chair in front of his desk and waited. Crossing her ankles to prevent her foot from tapping, she arranged her hands in her lap.

Stay calm. Remember, you're after the truth.

Whatever that might be.

Dana sat up straighter when Chief Gerard entered his office. He closed the door. She jumped before she could catch herself. Thankfully he didn't appear to notice. When he'd taken the seat behind his desk, he braced his elbows on the chair arms and steepled his fingers. Then he studied her at length.

She didn't look away. He represented the authority in this town. She was attempting to find the truth. He should be helping her not fighting her.

"Miss Dana, we have ourselves quite a dilemma here."

He paused for her to respond.

"I'm not sure I understand what you mean, Chief." Whatever he wanted to know he would have to ask. She wasn't giving anything voluntarily.

"Your mother's home burned. You and your friend, Mr. Spencer, have been going around upsetting the citizens of Brighton." He moved his head side to side. "I truly don't know what to do. I've issued verbal warnings and Mr. Spencer appears determined to ignore them."

"Talking to Lorie and the others this morning was my idea." Dana clamped her mouth shut. She'd said it. Let him think what he would. Spence was helping her. She intended to help him.

"I see." Gerard tapped his lips with his fingertips. "So, you're the one who's responsible for all the trouble."

The way he said the words…the way he looked at her. Fear crawled up her spine.

"Dana, I think it would be best if you went back to Chicago and put this behind you once and for all, just as I've told you already."

A blast of fury kicked aside the fear. "I'm not leaving until I know what happened." Okay, two could play this game. Dana leaned forward, braced her forearms on the edge of his desk. "You know what happened, Chief. Why don't you just tell me who you're covering for? I can't imagine why you'd conceal the identity of a killer, but somehow it feels exactly as if that's what you're doing."

Gerard pushed back from his desk and stood. "One of my deputies will come take your statement." He adjusted his utility belt. "The fire marshal wants to speak with you about the house." He stepped around his desk. "Get comfortable, Miss Hall, this might take a while."

EIGHT AND A HALF HOURS later, Chief Gerard allowed them to leave.

Dana felt ready to explode with frustration. She'd been questioned over and over about the fire…about every move she'd made since her arrival back in Brighton. Gerard hadn't even allowed her to eat lunch with Spence. One of the deputies had brought a sack lunch to her in the chief's office. That was where she'd stayed for the duration.

"Tell me about yours," Spence said as he started the car, "and I'll tell you about mine."

Dana smiled her first smile since waking up in his arms this morning.

She was getting entirely too comfortable with having him around.

"He asked me the same questions over and over. Who have we spoken to? What did we talk about?" She closed her eyes and tried to calm the whirlwind of questions and answers still ravaging her thought process. "What happened in the house prior to the fire? Etcetera. Etcetera."

"Ah," Spence said with an understanding nod, "I got that same script. Same questions asked fifty different ways."

All that and they didn't know any more than they had before they got here. No, that wasn't true. They knew there were secrets and lies...even in a small, refined town like Brighton.

Dana had to admit she was glad to see the motel. She was exhausted. A shower and sleep would be amazing.

"Get what you need from your room," Spence told her. "I'll order a pizza or something."

They'd decided she would be staying in his room, but she hadn't taken the time to get the rest of her stuff from room twelve yet.

Dana fished for the key in her purse. Spence waited for her to go into twelve before entering his room, eleven. She'd just closed the door when her gaze collided with a wild one staring directly at her.

She told herself to scream, but no sound came from her throat.

"Uh...sorry." Samuel Henagar, the former school janitor, pointed to the bathroom door. "Your toilet was running. I just came in here to fix it." He sidled around her to reach the door. "Wastes a lot of water running like that."

Dana remained frozen until he'd exited the room and she heard his footsteps echo all the way to the office.

The pathetic squeak that issued from her throat then made her want to kick something. A serial rapist could have been in here and Spence would never have known unless the rapist had made noise.

Dana had totally freaked.

She scrubbed her hand over her face and reminded herself that a shower would make her feel like a new woman.

She hoped so. She was getting pretty sick of the old one.

The telephone on the table beside the bed rang insistently. Dana pressed her hand to her chest. She was sick of being startled. She was sick of everything about this place.

She picked up the receiver. Prayed it wasn't her mother. "Hello."

"Meet me alone, and I'll tell you everything."

Female…Lorie. "Lorie?"

"I want this over."

Dana would have to be out of her mind to meet this woman alone. They'd known each other as kids, but they were all grown up now. Not to mention she never cared for Lorie's better-than-you attitude.

"Sorry, I can't meet you alone." Anticipation whipped through Dana. She wanted to know what those women knew. But she couldn't be stupid. "Mr. Spencer will have to be with me."

"Then I guess you'll never know the truth."

The simple statement echoed through Dana's soul.

"Why do we have to meet alone?"

Hesitation.

What if she'd changed her mind? Dana might have had a chance to know and blown it.

"I'll tell you everything, for your own information. Not for anyone else's. Alone. No negotiations."

"I'm not sure I can get out of here without him knowing," Dana confessed. There was only one door and that was right next to his.

"Climb out your bathroom window," Lorie ordered. "I'll pick you up in the back alley."

Two thoughts collided in Dana's brain just then. First, Lorie had definitely been the one to break into Dana's motel room. Second, this could be the biggest mistake of her life.

But she had to know.

If she learned the truth, it would be worth the risk.

Chapter Seventeen

Dana stared at the window for a whole minute before she could touch the lever that would open it. If she didn't hurry, Spence would be knocking on her door. She'd locked the door, but it wouldn't take him long to get the key and be inside. Or to knock it down.

She had to do this.

She had to be strong. This once.

Do it.

She opened the window, took a breath and climbed through.

It was a tight squeeze. She should have taken off her jacket.

Her hands hit the ground first.

Banging on the door to her room sent her heart cramming against her rib cage.

Hurry!

The rest of her body tumbled to the ground.

She scrambled up and ran.

Which way?

She scanned the dark alley.

Headlights came on to her right.

Run!

She didn't pause to think. She just ran.

She reached the front passenger door first.

"Get in the back!"

Ginger. She was in the front passenger seat.

Dana almost tripped getting to the back door. She wrenched the door open and threw herself in.

Tires spun and the car shot forward.

Dana glanced around the car as they passed under a streetlight. Patty was driving. Lorie was in the backseat with her.

They were all here.

The three girls who'd made her life miserable the weeks and months before her sister and the others died.

"Where are we going?" Dana hated that her voice sounded so small and weak. She wanted to be strong.

Ginger looked back at her. "You'll see."

SPENCE RAMMED his shoulder into the door. It didn't budge. Damn it.

Was she in the shower?

He shouted her name again.

Still no answer.

"What's going on here?"

He turned to find the motel manager hovering a few feet away.

"I need the key to this room."

Henagar reached for the ring of keys on his belt. "Won't do you no good to get in there." He rammed the key into the lock.

"Why do you say that?" Spence demanded. Frustration with a hefty dose of fear had already ignited inside him.

Henagar hitched his thumb behind him. "She went out the window into the alley. Got in a car with some other people and took off."

"Can you describe the car or the occupants?" Spence pushed the door open and went into the room.

"Nope." Henagar leaned on the doorjamb. "Too dark."

"You didn't get the license plate or anything?" Damn. Damn. Damn.

Henagar shook his head.

Dana's purse was on the bed. He checked it. Her cell phone was inside. No recent calls except for the three from her mother.

"Did you see which way they went at the end of the alley?"

Another indifferent shake of his head.

Of course not.

Spence walked to the bedside table and picked up the receiver. He entered the necessary numbers for the chief. Two rings and the other man's weary voice came across the line. "Gerard, we've got a problem." Spence wasn't going to waste time explaining what Henagar had just told him. "I'm at the motel. Dana Hall is missing."

The chief assured Spence he would be right there. Spence dropped the receiver back into its cradle. He turned back to Henagar. "And you didn't see anything else?"

"Didn't have to see nothing," Henagar said. "I know who it was."

Well, hell. "Who?" Spence demanded.

"The same ones who always had it in for Dana. The cheerleaders. They always picked on her. That sister of hers let 'em. Added fuel to the fire, if you ask me."

"Do you mean Lorie Hamilton, Ginger Ellis and Patty Shepard?" He'd known those three were hiding something.

Henagar nodded. "They always ran everything in school. If anyone gave 'em any trouble, they got their vengeance."

"What kind of vengeance?" Tension throbbed like a second heartbeat inside Spence. Memories of the little boy he'd helped rescue, only to have him returned to his mother, kept flickering one after the other inside his head. He wasn't having any repeats of the past.

Henagar shrugged. "They liked to embarrass the ones who didn't worship them. You know, make them sorry they were alive."

Spence could just imagine Dana—invisible, misunderstood Dana—being tortured by those bitches.

"Do you have any idea where they might take her?"

"Could be most anywhere. They're sneaky like that."

Spence walked back outside, set his hands on his hips and surveyed the deserted street. They could be anywhere.

And Dana was vulnerable.

She could break down completely…could end up dead.

Or, she could lash out.

Was that what happened sixteen years ago?

No. Spence shook his head slowly, firmly. Dana Hall didn't possess the necessary quality to kill anyone, not even in self-defense.

The killer was here though.

And it seemed a whole lot of people wanted to keep his or her identity a secret.

PATTY DROVE deep into the only cemetery in town.

Dana felt numb, but she wasn't afraid. She wasn't going to give them that much power. She had to be strong.

The car jerked to a stop and the women piled out. Dana got out a little slower. Take it slow, concentrate. This was her chance to learn the truth.

"We thought we'd visit your sister," Ginger said as she walked backward around the front of the car. "And her friends."

Dana's mouth was as dry as sand. Just words. *Words can't hurt you.*

Lorie came up behind Dana and pushed her toward the small, lonely headstone that belonged to her sister. She blinked back the tears. Her chest was so tight her heart could hardly beat. When her daddy had killed himself, her mother couldn't bear to come here and bury him next to Donna. Dana had been too numb to argue. She'd been a kid. Too much tragedy. Too much trauma.

She'd asked herself, though at the time, should she have killed herself? The pain would have stopped. But she'd never had the guts to do it.

She was a coward. She'd always been a coward.

"There." Ginger pointed to Donna's headstone. "See what you did."

Dana looked at her sister's eternal marker. *Beloved daughter...cherished sister.*

"That should've been you," Lorie snarled. "You were the one who hurt everything you touched."

Dana stared at the woman. As hard as she tried not to be injured by the words, they pierced straight through her heart. "I can't remember any of it." It was true. If she'd hurt someone's pet, she could not recall the act. Just like that night...the night her sister was murdered.

"Donna told us," Ginger shouted. "How can you keep pretending? Your own sister told us you killed Patty's cat." Her lips trembled. "She described in detail how you bragged to her about luring Pepper, my sweet puppy, into the woods behind your house." She shuddered visibly. "How could you do that to a poor helpless animal?"

Dana shook her head. "I was afraid of dogs." How could she have gone to Ginger's house and stolen her dog, walked it all the way back to her house and then...?

She didn't. That was the answer.

"Are you saying your sister lied?"

That wasn't possible. "No, I'm saying you're lying. Donna wouldn't have done that."

Ginger and Lorie laughed. "You're kidding, right?" Lorie demanded.

Dana didn't understand. None of this made sense.

"Your sister hated you," Ginger said. "She told us all about how pathetic you were. She didn't even like Sherry and Joanna. She only kept them around because they let her be the boss."

This was insane. "I don't believe you." Dana started to shake inside. They couldn't be right.

"Not long before she died, Donna said she was afraid of you."

Lorie couldn't be right. "She wouldn't have said that." Sharp, stabbing pains were hammering at Dana's head. She resisted the urge to squeeze her eyes shut against the building agony.

"We felt really bad for her when she didn't make the squad," Ginger said as she sat down on Donna's headstone. "But that's the breaks. She just wasn't good enough."

"She was so pathetic," Lorie chimed in. "We told her not to worry. If Sherry and Joanna died, she would be the only alternate."

Sherry and Joanna had died.

"Did you think you could make your sister love you if you cleared the way for her to be on the squad?" Ginger demanded.

"What?" Dana backed away a step. "This is insane."

"No," Lorie corrected. She pointed at Dana.

"You're insane. Donna was worried that you were re-sponsible. She was afraid to go to sleep at night in that room with you."

No. It wasn't that way at all. "You're wrong." The pain in her head had Dana rubbing at her temples. She shouldn't have come. All they had given her was lies. This couldn't be right.

"And then Patty conveniently fell down the stairs at school and broke her leg." Lorie claimed the step Dana had retreated. "That made room for an alternate to step up and be on the squad. Donna was the only alternate left."

Ginger stood, moved in next to Lorie. "The kids who saw it say you pushed her."

Dana couldn't hide her trembling now. She'd wanted to be strong. To stand up to whatever they threw her way. She was failing miserably. Her head was exploding.

"I didn't…" Dana turned to Patty. "I didn't push you. I didn't do any of this."

Patty just stared at her, looking almost as upset as Dana.

"The chief let you get away with killing three people," Lorie accused. "Just because he was friends with your father and felt sorry for your family. You were just a kid. How could they send you to prison? Your parents were already devastated."

"Death row is where they should have sent you," Ginger blasted. "You should just stop feigning amnesia, Dana. We all know the truth. You aren't the only one who wants this over. We've," she said as she banged on her chest, "tried to get on with our lives. But then you had to come back." She moved even closer to Dana. "Since you're here, you can make this right by going to the chief and telling him the truth."

This couldn't be right. It couldn't be.

Images of her holding that pillow…of pressing it down onto her sister's face exploded in Dana's brain.

Let me pretend to be you.

No, Donna, that's silly. I don't like it.

Frames of her childhood flashed like a movie reel before her eyes. Her and Donna running through the woods. Laughing. Playing games.

I'll be you and you be me.

Donna loved to fool people with that game.

"We're to blame, too," Patty abruptly shouted.

Lorie and Ginger glared at her.

Dana turned to the woman who had been quiet until then.

Patty sucked in a ragged breath. "If we hadn't joked and told Donna that she would be on the squad if…if Joanna and Sherry were out of the way…none of this would have happened."

"How were we—just kids—" Lorie shouted back

"—supposed to know she'd mention it to her psycho sister?" Lorie turned her furious gaze on Dana. "How could you do it? Sneak into their rooms while they were sleeping and suffocate them with their own pillows?"

The tidal wave of pain that washed through Dana's skull made her jerk. She tried to shake it off. "I don't know what you're talking about."

"Donna said—" Ginger picked up where Lorie left off "—that she read the details in your diary. She said you sat on top of Sherry and Joanna, held their arms down with your knees. You bragged that they barely struggled since you'd caught them in deep sleep."

"And when Donna was murdered," Lorie added, "your journal was conveniently missing."

The journal. Dana remembered the journal, but she didn't remember any of this. Why would Donna tell such things?

"We should have left Donna alone," Patty said, her face in her hands. "They're all three dead because we went too far."

"But now we're making up for it," Ginger suggested. "We'll make sure their killer is brought to justice. That'll make it right."

"Nothing will ever make it right," Patty shouted. "Don't you understand? Those girls are dead because we kept playing those stupid head games. This is our fault, too."

Dana closed her eyes. Tried to block the voices, the images.

This couldn't be right.

She couldn't have killed three people.

She couldn't have done all those other things.

But if she wasn't the one…that meant her sister was a liar…

And a killer.

Chapter Eighteen

Spence was waiting in the parking lot when the chief arrived. The man had scarcely gotten out of his car when Spence demanded, "Lorie Hamilton. Patty Shepard. Ginger Ellis." Spence cut through the air with his hand. "They're all involved in this. Dana's with them."

The startled expression that claimed the chief's face signaled that he understood this could turn out very badly. "How do you know she's with them?"

Why was this guy still pretending his citizens weren't dangerous? "Henagar saw them take Dana."

Gerard's gaze narrowed. "Did she go with them willingly?"

This was ridiculous! "Bottom line, Chief. Do you want another homicide to investigate?" The man blinked. "Because that's what you're going to get if we don't find them before someone snaps."

"You believe Dana is that close to the edge?"

Dana! It always came back to her. Couldn't the man see what was right in front of his face? *Calm down.* Spence had to remind himself of his boundaries in this case. He needed Gerard to cooperate. "Any one of those women could be teetering on the edge. There's something between them. Something about those murders. Right now, whatever that simmering issue is, it's about to detonate."

Gerard held up his hands. "All right. All right. We'll get a search under way. Check their homes. The scene where Donna's body was found. They can't have gone far. We'll find them."

Spence rounded the hood of the chief's car. "Let's start with the Hall home."

Gerard didn't argue. He put in the necessary calls to his deputies en route. The chief was right about one thing: Dana was on the edge. She'd carried this burden a very long time. She could very well snap. But she was not the only one.

On the edge or not, Spence wasn't ready to believe for a second that Dana was capable of murder.

But he couldn't say that about the other three.

Seven women, three were dead. One of the survivors could very well be responsible for the deaths of the others. The only question was, which one?

The sound of the chief's cell phone buzzing cut

through the tension building inside the car. He dragged it from his belt. "Gerard."

Spence clenched his jaw and waited out the call. The chief's curt responses gave away nothing.

When Gerard had closed his phone, he glanced at Spence. "Patty's car was found in a church parking lot."

"Abandoned?"

Gerard nodded. "No indication of a struggle or…anything else."

That was the way the search went. Ginger's SUV was at home. Lorie's minivan was in the elementary school parking lot. A precious hour had passed before Patty's mother was interviewed and related that her daughter had borrowed her car that afternoon.

The women had planned their little outing.

Not a good thing.

By the time Gerard and Spence had made it to the Hall property, he was damn worried. They had to find Dana. Now.

When the chief had surveyed the property around the charred remains of the house, he turned to Spence. "I don't think there's any point in stumbling around in those woods. There's no vehicle here. Wherever they are, they arrived in a car."

Spence's attention landed on the Bellomy house. A single light glimmered through a downstairs window. "We should check with the Bellomys. If anyone has been over here tonight, maybe they saw something."

Gerard shook his head. "The Bellomys go to bed pretty early. I doubt they're still up."

Spence wasn't about to let the chief's seeming indifference deter him. "I guess I'll find out."

"You're wasting our time, Mr. Spencer," Gerard called after him.

Spence kept walking. No one in this town appeared to get it. At least one person knew the truth and that one person was with three others who wanted that truth. Problem was, when the truth came out, Spence had a bad feeling it wasn't going to be what any of them expected.

He pounded on the front door twice before he heard stirring about inside.

"Mr. Spencer, I really don't think we should bother the Bellomys."

Spence ignored the chief who'd walked up behind him as he banged on the door a third time.

The night sounds amplified in the silence.

Spence was just about to bang on the door again when it opened. Mrs. Bellomy pushed her eyeglasses into place and peered out at the two men waiting on her porch. The robe she wore proclaimed the chief's accuracy about her having been in bed.

"Louise, I'm sure sorry about this," the chief began.

"Mrs. Bellomy," Spence interrupted, "is Mr. Bellomy home?"

Louise Bellomy looked from one man to the other. "What's going on? I…" Her gaze settled on Spence. "He's not in the bed. Has something happened?"

Spence turned to Gerard. "Have your deputies look for Mr. Bellomy's truck."

Mrs. Bellomy stepped out onto the porch. "Is his truck not in the garage?"

"I'll check, Louise."

The chief strode down the steps and across the yard. He was wasting his time. The truck wouldn't be there any more than Mr. Bellomy had been in the bed with his wife.

"Mrs. Bellomy, does your husband carry a cell phone?"

The lady shook her head. "I don't understand. What's happening?"

That was one question for which Spence would love the answer as well.

When the chief reappeared, he was on his phone giving his deputies the order to look for Bellomy's truck.

Spence turned to stare across the street at the sad remains of the Hall family's home.

Mr. Bellomy had lived right across the street sixteen years ago. He'd known Dana and Donna their whole lives. He'd likely seen things no one else had.

Did that make him friend or foe?

"GET THE BAG from the car," Ginger ordered, her gaze fixed on Dana.

"What're you doing, Ginger?" Patty asked, her attention divided between Dana and Ginger. She was nervous. Afraid.

Dana's headache had receded. She felt numb again. With the return of the numbness, the fear had vanished once more. Whatever these women decided to do to her she probably deserved.

If all they said was true…

"Just get it!" Ginger yelled at her friend. "I want this over."

Lorie ran to the car and scrounged around in the front seat. Patty backed away from where Ginger stood with Dana.

Dana was tired. Her knees felt ready to buckle. She did the only thing she felt able to do. She sat down on her sister's grave and waited on her fate.

She regretted very much that she had allowed Spence to believe in her. He would be disappointed when he learned that he'd made a mistake standing up for her.

Lorie thrust the backpack at Ginger. "What do you want me to do?"

A good friend to the end. Dana watched the women. She'd never had a friend like that. Even her sister had avoided her at school.

Dana had been alone.

Just like now.

"I'm telling you," Patty argued, "I'm not having any part in this. I'm calling Chief Gerard." She fished in her pocket for her phone.

"No you're not," Lorie commanded. She stalked up to her friend. "You're just as much a part of this as we are. You'll do what you have to. Then, this will finally be over."

"Or maybe," Ginger tossed out, "she wants the FBI to get involved. Then everyone will find out what we did."

Patty started to cry. "I can't do this. I just can't."

Dana almost felt sorry for her. She just wanted to go back home to her little house and her life. She didn't want to relive the past.

But what did Ginger mean "what they did"? Instinct tugged at Dana's failing reserve of fortitude.

Lorie pulled a notepad and a pen from the bag and tossed both onto Dana's lap. "Write your confession."

The three words rung in the night air.

"That's all you have to do," Lorie urged, her own fear showing now. "Then we'll call the chief and this will be over and we can all finally put it behind us."

"If you don't," Ginger said as she grabbed the bag from Lorie and pulled out a handgun, "then we'll… we'll use that concrete vase—" she used the gun to gesture to a nearby headstone "—to bash in your skull. The same way you did your sister's." The gun shook in her hand.

Dana's heart bumped against her sternum. She couldn't have done this! Why did they keep saying those awful things? She could probably get up and run. Ginger wouldn't shoot her. She was bluffing. She might be able to outrun Ginger and Lorie. Patty probably wouldn't even try to catch her.

But Dana wasn't going to. She wanted this over, too.

Her own sister had hated her enough to tell horrible lies on her.

A moment of clarity struck with life-shattering force.

Lies. That was what those stories had been. Dana hadn't hurt anyone's pets. She hadn't done any of that stuff they said she did.

Donna had lied.

Only the person who killed Sherry and Joanna would have known all the ugly details.

Images flashed in Dana's head. The pillow… Dana clasping it in her hands…holding it over her sister's face. *Die.*

If Donna killed Joanna and Sherry that would mean…that Dana killed her sister. That was the only explanation.

More of those terrifying images flashed one after the other. First she tried to suffocate her with the pillow…then she picked up the rock…

But Dana hadn't picked up a rock.

She'd been scared to death. Scrambling across the wet grass. Her nightgown had been plastered to her legs. She'd tried to get away.

"Put that gun down, Ginger."

All three of the women standing over Dana whipped around at the sound of the deep male voice.

Dana blinked. Mr. Bellomy? What was he doing here? Had he come to make things all right? The way he had that night.

Dana jerked with the memory.

She's alive! Everything's gonna be all right, honey.

"She has to tell the truth," Ginger argued. "Something has to be done!"

Mr. Bellomy glanced at Dana. "Just put the gun down, Ginger." When she didn't, he pleaded, "Put the gun down and *I'll* tell you the truth."

Dana tried to follow the conversation. Mr. Bellomy knew the truth?

Blue lights abruptly throbbed across the night, slicing the darkness.

"Oh, God, it's the police," Lorie murmured. She dropped the backpack.

Patty slumped to her knees and started sobbing.

The gun slipped from Ginger's hand. Plopped on the soft grass.

They were all staring at the police cruiser.

Except Dana. She stared at the gun. She lifted her gaze to the four standing around her, her gaze finally coming to rest on Mr. Bellomy.

He was the one to find her.

He couldn't have killed Donna…could he?

Her gaze settled on the gun once more.

Dana scrambled for the weapon.

She had it in her hand and was on her feet while the others were still watching Chief Gerard's approach.

Dana gripped the cold steel with both hands and leveled the barrel on Mr. Bellomy. "I want the truth."

Chapter Nineteen

Dana had a gun.

The slide of steel from leather warned that the chief had drawn his weapon even before Spence turned to see.

"Drop your weapon, Miss Hall," Gerard ordered.

"Just wait," Spence demanded.

Before the chief could respond, Spence strode as quickly as he dared toward the group gathered around Dana.

"Dana," he said softly, firmly as he cut between Ginger and Lorie. "Put the gun down. You don't want to do this."

"I want," Dana stated in a monotone voice that spoke of extreme fatigue and desperation, "the truth."

She was scared, confused and plain tired.

Gerard came closer. "You'd better listen to your friend, Dana."

Spence wished like hell that the chief would lower his weapon. But deep down he understood why he hadn't. "Dana," Spence urged, "one wrong move… one twitch of your finger could set off a chain reaction that none of us wants. Please, lower the weapon."

Her hands shook, but she didn't do as he asked.

"Tell 'em, Waylon," Bellomy said to Gerard. "Tell 'em all. What difference does it make now?"

Spence made a decision at that moment. He was going to show Dana Hall that someone trusted her… believed in her.

"Dana," he said gently. "I'm going to take the gun because I know—" he put his hand to his chest "—that you would never hurt anyone." Then he reached out. "I'm going to take the gun and then the chief is going to tell us the truth, so this nightmare will be over."

Dana's gaze collided with his. The hope, the desperation he saw there tore him apart inside.

Slowly, just a few inches at a time, he moved toward her. He wrapped his fingers around the muzzle of the weapon and pulled it free of her grasp. She dropped her hands to her sides and shuddered visibly.

When Spence had tucked the weapon into his waistband, he moved in closer, put his arm around her and let her lean against him.

"Now," he said to Gerard who had lowered his weapon as well, "we want the truth."

Gerard holstered his weapon. He glanced at Bellomy, who nodded for him to do as Spence asked.

"We believe," Gerard began, "that Donna was a very ill little girl. Her father didn't realize how much so until it was too late."

Dana trembled. Spence held her tighter.

"I don't understand," she protested.

Her voice was thin, shaky. Spence wished there was more he could do…something to spare her the painful reality that was no doubt to come.

"My old hound dog went missing," Bellomy took up where the chief left off. "It was days before I found him." He shook his head. "And when I did, Donna was there. I'd been watching her go off into the woods alone. I followed her. She swore she wasn't the one who killed him. She found him and buried him. But decided to come back and dig him up and make sure she hadn't dreamed the whole thing. And—" he shook his head "—I wanted to believe her, so I did." He moved his head sadly from side to side. "There were other things. Couple of our neighbors had pets go missing. We all figured it was just one of those things."

"She was the one to do those awful things to your cat," the chief said to Patty. "Her father found her writing about it in Dana's diary. She insisted Dana had written it and that she was trying to mark it out so no one would know. She was afraid you'd be in trouble. Your daddy couldn't be sure and, like Carlton, he wanted to believe her. Later he realized he'd been wrong."

"And my dog," Ginger spoke up. "Did she hurt him?"

Even after sixteen years, emotion glistened in the woman's eyes.

Chief Gerard nodded. "Donna did a lot of terrible, terrible things." Gerard settled his gaze back on Dana. "She killed Joanna and Sherry. She wrote about that in your diary, too. To make you look guilty. We didn't find out until later. Your father thought he'd hidden the diary, but she evidently found it."

Dana moistened her lips and took a breath. "How can you be sure she lied about the journal?"

She was still afraid her nightmares might hold some truth.

"And who killed Donna?" Patty got to her feet, swiped her damp cheeks. "None of this answers that question."

Bellomy and Gerard exchanged a look.

"Understand," Gerard said with a pointed look at each person present, "we were reeling from two murders. It hadn't been a week since we'd found those girls dead in their beds. There hadn't been time to put two and two together. We were all stunned when we finally put it all together."

"Your father woke up that night," Bellomy explained. "Maybe he heard the back door slam. Or maybe his instincts had been nagging him, even in his sleep. He got up to check on you girls and you were missing. When your daddy considered that two girls were dead and Donna had been torturing and killing animals for months, it somehow all broke through the fog of denial. He rushed out of the house to try and find the two of you."

Dana couldn't believe what she was hearing. Her sister had killed her two best friends. She'd harmed all those animals. God, how was that possible?

"I got the call just an hour or so later."

This didn't make sense. "If my father found us, why the search party? The whole thing was in the papers. People looked for hours." Dana didn't have to remember that part. She'd read all about it in the papers.

Gerard nodded. "Two hours to be exact."

"When your mother woke up and found everyone missing," Mr. Bellomy explained, "she rushed outside to see what was going on. Your father had walked back to the house. He was in shock. He kept saying *the girls…something happened to the girls… they went into the woods*. Your mother called the chief, then rushed over to get me. By the time we got back over to your house, your father was shut up in your room. I sent your mother out to watch for the chief and I begged your daddy to talk to me."

Dana held her breath.

"He—" Bellomy's shoulders sagged in defeat "—said he went to the stream looking for the two of you when he woke up and found you missing. He knew you liked going there. When he found the two of you, Donna was in the process of smothering you with a pillow. Your father said he didn't even think; he just acted. He rushed over and pulled her off you. She fought him, kept trying to get to you. He pushed her away so he could see if you were still breathing. I guess he pushed harder than he meant to. She fell… hit her head."

"Donna was dead," Spence guessed.

Bellomy nodded. "He was beside himself. Thought you were both dead. Something inside him just shut off and he walked back to the house to get help. But he was so disoriented he couldn't get the facts straight." Bellomy blew out a heavy breath. "When I found him in your room, he had his shotgun ready to kill himself. I begged him to let me go to where you were and see if maybe he'd misjudged the situation. He finally relented. I left him with your mother, and I grabbed the closest deputy and headed into the woods. The chief sent the others who'd showed up to search in different directions all over those woods."

"When he got to the stream," Gerard said, "Donna was dead. According to the autopsy the injury killed her pretty much instantly. Just the right pressure in just the right place. Nothing your daddy could've done would have saved her."

"But you were alive," Bellomy said. "When I carried you back to the house, your daddy fell to his knees and cried like a baby."

"But it ate at him," Dana said. "The truth ate at him until he couldn't live with it any longer."

Somber silence was her only response.

"None of this is in the case file," Spence said to Gerard.

The chief shook his head. "What was the point? It wasn't murder. The murderer was dead. Donna's death was an accident. There was nothing to be gained by dragging the Hall family through that kind of ordeal. It was better that no one ever knew."

"Was it?" Dana stepped away from Spence.

"Some had to live with the questions and the doubts," Lorie added.

"Some of us," Dana trumped her statement, "were never able to live at all."

Gerard stared at the ground. There was nothing he could say.

Sixteen years ago Brighton's chief of police had made a decision to protect a family from being further devastated.

And all involved had suffered the consequences ever since.

Chapter Twenty

Dana stood on the street and reflected on what remained of her childhood home.

It was finally over.

The newspapers and media networks were in a frenzy over the breaking story.

But at least everyone knew the truth.

Dana hadn't killed anyone. In her nightmares she had relived her sister trying to kill her over and over. Since her sister was the one who ended up dead, Dana's mind had twisted the memories, making her believe she'd been the one doing the killing.

Patty, Lorie and Ginger had come to terms with the reality that their game playing was merely the final straw culminating in the complete break from reality of an already damaged mind. That was something the three of them would have to live with the rest of their lives.

Dana's mother had never known the truth. She was stunned, but the truth explained a lot. She had spent fifteen years blaming herself for her husband's suicide. Now she knew it hadn't been about her or their marriage. It had been about his inability to live with the fact that if he'd acted sooner, stepped out of denial a little faster, Joanna, Sherry and Donna all might have lived. But it hadn't been his fault. He'd loved his daughters. He'd made a very human mistake.

"You ready to head back to Chicago?"

Dana turned to Spence. She smiled. He had believed in her when no one else dared. She was immensely thankful her search for the truth had brought them together.

"Yes. I am so ready."

He hesitated. "I was thinking that maybe since you're not officially my client anymore...maybe we could go to dinner." He shrugged. "Maybe catch a movie."

Dana's smile broadened to a grin. "The answer is yes. I would like that very much."

He leaned down and placed a sweet, chaste kiss on her cheek. She tiptoed, captured his lips with her own before he could pull away. She was ready for far more. For a real kiss.

Finally, Dana Hall was ready for a real life.

Chapter Twenty-One

Chicago, Illinois

Victoria hugged her granddaughter closer to her side.

Jamie had fallen asleep before they were out of the parking lot. Dinner and a movie had been the perfect ending for this stressful week.

"Let's take the long way home this time, Neal."

"Yes, ma'am. The long way it is." The driver flashed her a smile in the rearview mirror. As per her instructions, he didn't take the usual roads.

Victoria didn't have to turn back and look to know her security detail would be close behind. That was another stressor for her granddaughter. Even as young as she was, the child had noticed the additional personnel at the house and the fact that a driver took them everywhere, including to school lately.

But Victoria was taking no chances with her granddaughter's safety.

Thankfully Lucas would be home next week. Two weeks after that, Jim and Tasha would be heading back as well. Victoria wouldn't relax until she had her whole family around her. She had complete confidence in every member of her staff, but she needed her husband and her son close until this was finished.

Nothing had turned up on the search for intelligence related to the threat to Victoria and her grandchild. But she was not foolish enough to believe the threat held no merit. No matter that the school officials had insisted that the occasional freak incident happened causing the alarm system to react, Victoria was not convinced.

She smoothed a hand through Jamie's silky blond hair. This child would never experience what her father had suffered. Victoria would see to that.

No matter the sacrifice or the cost.

Jamie Colby would be protected.

The streets of Chicago were quiet tonight.

Victoria turned her attention to the city she loved so much. Her life, with all its pain as well as its glory, had played out in this dynamic city.

The Colby Agency had made its home here and put down deep, deep roots. Desperate souls from across the nation came through the agency's doors and all received the help and relief they sought.

Like Dana Hall. She now had her life back. She could begin anew with the truth on her side.

Spence had done a fine job. Victoria was certainly pleased to have him on staff. Merrilee Walters would arrive tomorrow. Victoria looked forward to the challenge of helping her fit in.

A traffic light changed, and the car slowed to a stop. Jamie snuggled deeper into her grandmother's arms. Victoria smiled. The freedom of pure innocence. She prayed the future would hold the best life had to offer for the sweet child.

Some would say it was the hard times that made the good ones all the sweeter. Perhaps so. Victoria took the bad with the good and hoped for the best.

Always, always, however, she braced for the worst.

The squeal of tires drew her attention forward. As the traffic light turned green, a car traveling on the cross street skidded to a stop in their path.

"For the love of—"

Glass shattered, cutting short the driver's words. His head jerked back, and something wet splattered across Victoria's face.

The gaping hole in the back of his head didn't fully register until she swiped her face and saw the red on her hand.

Blood.

More gunshots pierced the night. Her security detail was returning fire outside her car.

Victoria lunged into action. She settled Jamie on the floor, used her body as a shield above her and whispered assurances to the child. She reached beneath her jacket, her fingers seeking—

The sound of something metal scraping glass alerted Victoria that someone was at her door, jimmying the lock. She could still hear the exchange of gunfire outside. Her heart rocketed into her throat.

As the door wrenched open, Victoria's hand came from under her jacket; she twisted her torso and leveled the barrel of the Ruger on the man's ski-mask-clad face. "Drop that weapon or I will blow your head off."

"Give me the kid and I'll let you live," he growled, the barrel of his Glock aimed at her forehead.

"Close the door and walk away," Victoria countered, "and I'll let *you* live."

The pop of gunshots outside had slowed like a bag of microwave popcorn nearing ready, but it wasn't done yet.

The man laughed. "Look, you old bitch, give me the kid *now* or you're dead."

"Wrong answer." Victoria sent a bullet straight through his brain.

The man crumpled onto the seat. Victoria snatched the gun from his fingers. She wanted to check his ID, but she didn't dare move. Whatever was going on outside wasn't over. She had to stay down…had to protect Jamie.

Fully awake now, Jamie whimpered.

"It's okay, baby." Victoria rocked her as best she could in their awkward position. And she prayed… that God would see them safely through this.

"Victoria, are you all right?"

Her head came up and relief flooded her at the sight of Ian's face.

"You can come out now." He offered a hand to assist her. "We've neutralized the situation out here."

This time.

Victoria eased back up into the seat, pulling Jamie with her.

But what about next time?

If they didn't learn the source of this threat soon…

All the enemy needed was one moment, one tiny slip in security.

Victoria had to make sure they didn't get it.

* * * * *

Look for the next installment in the
COLBY AGENCY:
ELITE RECONNAISSANCE DIVISION *trilogy*
next month!
Here's an excerpt from:
THE BRIDE'S SECRETS
by
Debra Webb
Available August wherever
Harlequin Books are sold.

Chapter One

The Colby Agency's conference room overflowed with staff members. All were present for this morning's meeting, except the newest investigator on staff. He had taken a bullet last night while serving on Victoria's personal security detail.

Victoria Colby-Camp sat at the head of the long table, listening as Ian Michaels reviewed the tightened security measures. Last night's attack had confirmed the worst.

The risk to her granddaughter's safety was no longer mere theory or rumor. It was real.

Too real.

Increasing fear pumped through Victoria's veins with every frantic beat of her heart. Nothing she or her people had done so far had given them the answers for which they searched.

Every lead turned into a dead end.

Yet, someone out there continued to attempt to get to her granddaughter.

Her loyal staff began filing out of the room. Victoria blinked, dragged her focus back to the present. She hadn't realized Ian had concluded his briefing.

Ian settled in a chair to her right; Simon Ruhl did the same on her left.

Time for the postmortem. These two men were Victoria's most trusted associates, professional and personal. Yet, like her, they could only react to the threat. Whoever was behind this had burrowed so deeply beneath multiple ambiguous layers of disinformation that it would take time—precious time—to ferret them out.

This was the first occasion in the Colby Agency's prestigious history that Victoria had no choice but to admit that they were mystified.

"Last night," Simon kicked off the overview of the little known facts, "an attempt was made to abduct Jamie."

The sound of a bullet shattering the windshield, killing the driver, echoed through Victoria's mind. Three were dead, including two unidentified males involved in the abduction attempt. Two others had fled the scene. The newest member of her trusted staff had been injured. J.T. Baxley had taken a bullet. Though he'd been treated and released, the risk to his life—to her granddaughter's—had shaken Victoria to the core.

"Have we learned anything new?" Otherwise she saw no need to go over these horrendous details yet again. Another image, this one of her pulling the trigger, ending the life of the man with the gun in her face, erupted in her mind.

She'd had no choice…and still, the realization deeply disturbed her.

Rather than answering her question, Ian and Simon exchanged a long look. Now she understood.

"You believe it's an inside job." It pained Victoria to say the words.

"Yes," Ian confirmed.

"That's the only way anyone could have known your schedule for last evening," Simon clarified. "None of us want to believe that's possible."

"At this point—" Ian picked up where Simon left off "—we have to face that undeniable possibility."

Victoria took a breath; her chest tightened with the emotions charging through her. "Do you have a suspect?"

Her closest confidants shared another look.

She wasn't going to like their conclusion. Victoria wasn't happy with the concept in general, but obviously the answer was going to be even less palatable than it already was.

"J.T. Baxley," Ian stated.

J.T.? "I was at his christening." Victoria had just graduated from the university at the time. One of her dearest friends had opted marriage over college and J.T. was her first and only child.

Simon nodded his understanding. "We fully understand that you've known J.T. and his family for years. But he was one of the few who had access to last night's schedule."

That was true. J.T. had been a part of her security detail last night. And he'd paid the price.

Victoria shook her head. "This simply isn't possible." She had sought out J.T. when his mother had relayed that he had left the insurance industry. Victoria had hoped for years that she would be able to lure him to the Colby Agency. Only a few months ago that opportunity had arisen. He'd signed on as a member of her Elite Reconnaissance Division.

"J.T. ignored the all-hands call this morning."

Their announcement sent a new kind of fear throttling through Victoria. "Has anyone checked on him?" The man had been shot, for God's sake. Though the shot appeared to have been clean, in and out of the bicep with no apparent serious damage, there was always the chance something had been missed. She'd thought nothing of his absence considering what he'd gone through last night.

"I went to his apartment myself," Ian assured her. "He wasn't there. There was no indication he'd slept in his bed. Nothing appeared to be missing. His cell phone was on the kitchen counter, and his car was in the parking garage."

"Then we should be concerned for his safety, not suspicious of his participation in this deception," Victoria argued. The suggestion was preposterous.

"J.T. may not have been a willing participant," Simon qualified. "We've learned some unsettling details regarding his former fiancée."

A frown worried Victoria's brow. J.T. had been devastated when his bride hadn't shown. He'd literally been left at the altar. That had been only two weeks ago. Victoria had allowed him to focus on trying to find out what happened to the woman who seemed to have simply vanished rather than take on another agency assignment. The agony of watching his desperation play out tortured her even now as she considered his plight.

"Explain," Victoria prompted.

"We don't have in-depth details as of yet," Ian offered. "But we have uncovered a number of aliases she has operated under during the past six or seven years. From all appearances, Eve Mattson is a serious scam artist. She may have been playing J.T. as a part of setting the stage for Jamie's abduction."

Victoria looked from Ian to Simon. "Find J.T. Whoever this Eve Mattson is or was, we owe it to J.T. to give him the benefit of the doubt. If he's in trouble, we'll back him up."

J.T. was her friend's only son—only child period. Victoria would not let him down. If he had somehow been drawn into this plan against Victoria's granddaughter, it would have been unknowingly and certainly unwillingly.

"Also, find out who Eve Mattson is," Victoria went on. "I promised J.T. I wouldn't interfere with his search for his missing bride-to-be, but this changes everything. If Eve Mattson is involved in the plan to harm my granddaughter, I want her found and the truth extracted." Fury detonated inside Victoria. "Whoever is behind this is going to rue the day they picked the Colby Agency as a target."

If it was the last thing Victoria did, all involved would pay the fiddler a hefty price for this dance.

We'll be spotlighting a different series every month throughout 2009 to celebrate our 60th anniversary.

LOOK FOR HARLEQUIN INTRIGUE® IN AUGUST!

To commemorate the event, Harlequin Intrigue® is thrilled to invite you to the wedding of the Colby Agency's J.T. Baxley and his bride, Eve Mattson.

Look for *Colby Agency: Elite Reconnaissance*

THE BRIDE'S SECRETS
BY DEBRA WEBB

Available August 2009

www.eHarlequin.com

HARLEQUIN® Romance®

Welcome to the intensely emotional world of

MARGARET WAY

with

Cattle Baron: Nanny Needed

It's a media scandal! Flame-haired beauty
Amber Wyatt has gate-crashed her ex-fiancé's
glamorous society wedding. Groomsman
Cal McFarlane knows she's trouble, but when
Amber loses her job, the rugged cattle rancher
comes to the rescue. He needs a nanny, and
if it makes his baby nephew happy, he's
willing to play with fire....

*Available in August
wherever books are sold.*

You're invited to join our Tell Harlequin Reader Panel!

By joining our new reader panel you will:

- Receive Harlequin® books—they are FREE and yours to keep with no obligation to purchase anything!
- Participate in fun online surveys
- Exchange opinions and ideas with women just like you
- Have a say in our new book ideas and help us publish the best in women's fiction

In addition, you will have a chance to win great prizes and receive special gifts! See Web site for details. Some conditions apply. Space is limited.

To join, visit us at

www.TellHarlequin.com.

REQUEST YOUR FREE BOOKS!

2 FREE NOVELS PLUS 2 FREE GIFTS!

HARLEQUIN®

INTRIGUE®

Breathtaking Romantic Suspense

YES! Please send me 2 FREE Harlequin Intrigue® novels and my 2 FREE gifts (gifts are worth about $10). After receiving them, if I don't wish to receive any more books, I can return the shipping statement marked "cancel." If I don't cancel, I will receive 6 brand-new novels every month and be billed just $4.24 per book in the U.S. or $4.99 per book in Canada. That's a savings of close to 15% off the cover price! It's quite a bargain! Shipping and handling is just 50¢ per book.* I understand that accepting the 2 free books and gifts places me under no obligation to buy anything. I can always return a shipment and cancel at any time. Even if I never buy another book from Harlequin, the two free books and gifts are mine to keep forever.

182 HDN EYTR 382 HDN EYT3

Name	(PLEASE PRINT)	

Address		Apt. #

City	State/Prov.	Zip/Postal Code

Signature (if under 18, a parent or guardian must sign)

Mail to the **Harlequin Reader Service:**
IN U.S.A.: P.O. Box 1867, Buffalo, NY 14240-1867
IN CANADA: P.O. Box 609, Fort Erie, Ontario L2A 5X3

Not valid to current subscribers of Harlequin Intrigue books.

Are you a current subscriber of Harlequin Intrigue books and want to receive the larger-print edition? Call 1-800-873-8635 today!

* Terms and prices subject to change without notice. Prices do not include applicable taxes. Sales tax applicable in N.Y. Canadian residents will be charged applicable provincial taxes and GST. Offer not valid in Quebec. This offer is limited to one order per household. All orders subject to approval. Credit or debit balances in a customer's account(s) may be offset by any other outstanding balance owed by or to the customer. Please allow 4 to 6 weeks for delivery. Offer available while quantities last.

Your Privacy: Harlequin is committed to protecting your privacy. Our Privacy Policy is available online at www.eHarlequin.com or upon request from the Reader Service. From time to time we make our lists of customers available to reputable third parties who may have a product or service of interest to you. If you would prefer we not share your name and address, please check here. ☐

HI09R

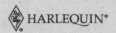
HARLEQUIN®

INTRIGUE°

COMING NEXT MONTH

Available August 11, 2009

#1149 STEALING THUNDER by Patricia Rosemoor
The McKenna Legacy

Fearing his love is a curse, the charming cowboy avoids relationships—until he meets the one woman he can't live without. Now someone is threatening her life, and there is nothing he wouldn't do to protect her.

#1150 MORE THAN A MAN by Rebecca York
43 Light Street

His bride knows that her protective billionaire is no ordinary man, but she doesn't know all of his secrets. Can he trust her with the truth and shield her from his enemies?

#1151 THE BRIDE'S SECRETS by Debra Webb
Colby Agency: Elite Reconnaissance Division

A Colby Agency P.I. discovers that there is more to the woman he meant to marry than meets the eye, and he won't rest until he knows whether their relationship was a lie. But first he must find his runaway bride.

#1152 COWBOY TO THE CORE by Joanna Wayne
Special Ops Texas

He spent years serving his country in a special ops unit, but now this military man longs to return to his cowboy ways. Back home in Texas, his dreams of the quiet life are shattered when he meets a woman in danger…a woman who rouses all his protective instincts.

#1153 FAMILIAR SHOWDOWN by Caroline Burnes
Fear Familiar

Betrayed by her presumed dead—and double agent—fiancé, the ranch manager won't let another man lie to her. Now she learns that her new hire is really an undercover agent, and he's looking for the truth. Well, so is she! Will he be the last straw or her salvation?

#1154 NAVAJO COURAGE by Aimée Thurlo
Brotherhood of Warriors

To catch a serial killer, her department brings in a Navajo investigator. Although she may not agree with his methods, she can't ignore his unique skills or his sensuous touch. But the killer may be closer than they think….

www.eHarlequin.com